Clutch Hitter

The Chip Hilton Sports Series

For more information on
Chip Hilton-related activities and to correspond
with other Chip fans, check the Internet at
chiphilton.com

Chip Hilton Sports Series
#4

Clutch Hitter

Coach Clair Bee
Updated by Randall and Cynthia Bee Farley
Foreword by Bobby Knight

BROADMAN
& HOLMAN
PUBLISHERS

Nashville, Tennessee

0-8054-1817-2

Published by Broadman & Holman Publishers,
Nashville, Tennessee
Senior Acquisitions & Development Editor:
William D. Watkins
Page Design: Anderson Thomas Design, Nashville, Tennessee
Typesetting: PerfecType, Nashville, Tennessee

Subject Heading: BASEBALL—FICTION / YOUTH
Library of Congress Card Catalog Number: 98-28093

Library of Congress Cataloging-in-Publication Data
Bee, Clair.
    Clutch hitter / Clair Bee ; edited by Cynthia Bee Farley
and Randall K. Farley.
        p. cm. — (Chip Hilton sports series ; v. 4)
    Updated ed. of a work published in 1949.
    Summary: While playing baseball for the steel company
where he works during the summer, high school star athlete
Chip Hilton comes up against professionals participating
illegally in amateur sport.
    ISBN 0-8054-1817-2 (alk. paper)
    [1. Baseball—Fiction. 2. Sportsmanship—Fiction.]
I. Farley, Cynthia Bee, 1952– . II. Farley, Randall K.,
1952– . III. Title. IV. Series: Bee, Clair. Chip Hilton sports
series ; v. 4.

PZ7.B38196Cl   1998
[Fic]—dc21   98-28093
                                                       CIP
                                                        AC

1 2 3 4 5 02 01 00 99 98

TO MY SON

CLAIR FRANCIS "BOBO" BEE

Who arrived during the writing of this story and who,
a proud father hopes, will love baseball with
all of the devotion and fervor of his namesake.

COACH CLAIR F. BEE, 1949

TO

DEAN SMITH

CLAIR BEE'S GOOD FRIEND

A true gentleman and sportsman whose life proves
nice guys do finish first—
and, in Coach Smith's case, more often than any other
coach in the history of the game!

RANDY, CINDY, AND MICHAEL FARLEY, 1998

Contents

CONTENTS

Foreword

THE IS nothing that could be a greater honor for me than to be able to write the foreword to the new editions of the Chip Hilton books written by Clair Bee and revised by his daughter Cindy and son-in-law Randy.

I can remember that in the early and midfifties, when I was in junior high and high school, there was nothing more exciting, outside of actually playing a game, than reading one of the books from Coach Bee's Chip Hilton series. He wrote twenty-three books in all, and I bought and read each one of them during my student days. His books were about the three sports that I played—football, basketball, and baseball—and had the kind of characters in them that every young boy wanted to imagine that he was or could become.

Chip Hilton himself was a combination of everything that was good, right, and fair in athletic competition. His accomplishments on the field, on the floor, or on the diamond were the things that made every boy's dreams.

CLUTCH HITTER

Henry Rockwell was the kind of coach that every boy wanted to play for, and he knew how to get the best out of every boy who played for him.

My mother and grandmother used to take me shopping with them in Akron and would leave me at the bookstore in O'Neil's department store with $1.25 to purchase the Chip Hilton book of my choice. It would invariably take me at least two hours to decide which of these wonderfully vivid episodes in athletic competition, struggle, and accomplishment I would purchase.

As I read my way through the entire series, I learned there was a much greater value to what Clair Bee had written than just the lifelike portrayal of athletic competition. His books had a tremendous sense of right and wrong, what was fair and what wasn't, and what the word *sportsmanship* was all about.

During the first year I was at the United States Military Academy at West Point as an assistant basketball coach, I had the opportunity to meet Clair Bee, the author of those great stories that were such an integral part of my boyhood dreams. After all, no boy could have ever read those wonderful stories without imagining himself as Chip Hilton.

Clair Bee became one of the two most influential people in my career as a college coach. I have never met a man whose intelligence I have admired more. No one person has ever contributed more to the game of basketball in the development of the fundamental skills, tactics, and strategies of the game than Clair Bee during his fifty years as a teacher of the sport. I strongly believe that the same can be said of his authorship of the Chip Hilton series.

It seems that every day I am asked by a parent, "What can be done to interest my son in sports?" Or "What is the best thing I can do for my son, who really has shown an interest in sports?" For the past thirty-three years, when I have been asked those questions, I have always answered by saying, "Have your son read about Chip Hilton." Then I've explained a little bit about the Chip Hilton series.

The enjoyment that a young athlete can get from reading the Chip Hilton series is just as great today as it was for me more than forty years ago. The lessons that Clair Bee teaches through Chip Hilton and his exploits are the most meaningful and priceless examples of what is right and fair about life that I have ever read. I have the entire series in a glass case in my library at home. I still spend a lot of hours browsing through those twenty-three books.

As a coach, I will always be indebted to Clair Bee for the many hours he spent helping me learn about the game of basketball. As a person, I owe an even greater debt to him for providing me with the most memorable reading of my youth through his series on Chip Hilton.

BOB KNIGHT
Head Coach, Men's Basketball, Indiana University

CHAPTER 1

The New Hurler

WILLIAM "CHIP" HILTON'S gray eyes flickered toward the dugout where a laughing, talking group of players dressed in the road uniforms of the Mansfield Steelers were swinging bats and waiting for their turn at the plate. Chip's glance went toward the on-deck circle where the next hitter stood listening to a stocky, middle-aged man who was wearing white practice pants and a dusty, gray sweat shirt. The hitter was gently hefting a long bat as he listened to the team manager's instructions.

Jim "Gunner" Kirk, a former catcher, had never quite made the big leagues, but he had played in organized baseball for years. His disposition was rough, and on the field, much of his speech was profane. The burly manager was not the type of man a teenager like Chip Hilton could respect; he was not the kind of coach Chip had ever known during his young athletic career. Now, Kirk accentuated each word with the gnarled forefinger of his right hand as he spoke in low tones to the batter.

CLUTCH HITTER

"I wanna see what this kid's got, understand? Make him throw it in there! Got it? Pass the word along to the other guys when you've had your swings. No reachin' now! It's gotta be right in there!"

Chip Hilton couldn't hear what the manager was saying, but his intuition told him that he was probably a part of that conversation. He was, after all, a teenager playing against seasoned adults, and he could expect a good going-over. Chip's thoughts returned to his talk with Coach Henry Rockwell just two days earlier. It was the day he had taken his English exam at Valley Falls High School, and Rockwell had relayed to him a summer job offer.

"First impressions are most lasting, Chip," Rockwell had said, "so you just take everything in stride and be a good sport. You're going up to Mansfield for the summer to get a little baseball experience and earn some money. I'm not worried about the working part; you've worked nearly all your life. But the baseball aspect is another matter.

"I've known H. L. Armstrong for forty years. He's a great person in every respect. He worked his way up step by step to the presidency of the company, but he never got too important to forget his love for sports—especially baseball! The Mansfield Steel Company fields amateur teams in about every sport, and H. L. is about the best supporter the team has. You'll like him!

"Now for your part as a member of the team. H. L. asked me to send him a good pitcher for the summer because he's got his heart set on winning the championship of the Mansfield Industrial Baseball Association. I don't know much about Kirk, the man he's got managing his club, so I want you to be careful and take care of that arm of yours. Remember, you've got another year here at

THE NEW HURLER

Valley Falls High School, and then, I hope, four years at State. A young pitcher like you should have at least three days' rest between games. I want you to promise me you won't pitch more often. OK? Work hard. See you in early September."

Then Valley Falls's veteran high school coach had clapped Chip fondly on the shoulder and said good-bye. "Good luck, Chipper," he had said softly, "and remember, take care of that arm!"

"All right, pretty boy, let's go!"

The sarcastic voice of Buster Dillon snapped Chip back to reality, and he toed the rubber and aimed the ball at the bulky receiver's target. The pitch was shoulder-high, and the tall hitter met the ball solidly. Chip didn't have to look around to know that ball had really been tagged; it was over the fence, one for the kids waiting outside Steeler Park.

Gunner Kirk, standing behind the mound where he could watch Chip's pitches, dug another ball out of the bag he held.

"Come on, kid," he growled, "put something on it!"

Behind the plate, Buster Dillon, his chunky body encased in full catcher's gear, shifted his feet impatiently and thumped his big glove.

"What is this?" he rasped. "Volleyball? You ain't throwin' hard enough to break a pane of glass!"

Dillon's snide comments were greeted with a few chuckles and smiles from the players in front of the dugout, but Chip noticed they were not too enthusiastic. Although this was Chip's first practice with the team, he could already sense that Dillon wasn't popular with the rest of the players. Buster's tongue was sharp and cutting. He was constantly bickering, riding, or mocking someone. Even Gunner Kirk, the team manager and Dillon's friend and constant baseball companion, came in for a bit of razzing now and then from the grouchy receiver.

Chip's ears burned a little, but he gave no other sign that he resented Dillon's taunting. He toed the rubber, took a full windup, and sent a straight hard one across the letters on the hitter's shirt. But the throw was just slightly outside the strike zone, and the batter let it go by with a wry smile; he liked that kind of a pitch.

Dillon grunted his disgust and nearly tore the glove off Chip's hand on the return throw. "Come on, Mabel," he yelled sarcastically. "Throw the little ball hard—at least once, if you can!"

But if Buster Dillon thought he was going to get a rise out of Chip Hilton, he had another thought coming. A slight smile crossed the tall, blond hurler's lips as he again took a full windup and sent the next ball across the heart of the plate. There wasn't much on the pitch, and the hitter teed off, sending a long line drive to the left-field fence.

As the players took their turns at the plate, Chip had the chance to look them over carefully, and he tried to figure out their batting weaknesses. He also wondered just what kind of person each one was. Most of the players were older men, but a few were just a little older than Chip. They held regular full-time jobs with the Mansfield Steel Company. Additionally, a few players, like Chip, were working only during the summer months and were considered part-time employees, but they were still eligible to play in the prestigious industrial league. The older men were past their baseball prime but seemed to enjoy every minute of the practice, even though the workout was held after the regular day's work in the mills. Tired as they might be, anyone could see the work-weariness disappear as they played. They loved baseball.

THE NEW HURLER

Chip knew one of the Steelers players, not personally, but by his baseball reputation. Richard "Duck" Tucker was a senior at the state university and was pitching summer ball for the Mansfield Steelers for the second-straight season. He was good too. Chip had read that a number of major-league scouts were just waiting for Tucker to finish his college career so they could try to sign him to a professional contract. Tucker had one more year of college baseball to play before his graduation. But no matter how good Duck Tucker was on the mound, he was anything but a good sport in the dressing room with a newcomer.

Chip had arrived in Mansfield that morning and had been met by Gunner Kirk at the airport. After lunch, he had accompanied Kirk to the big steel mill and gone through all the usual new employee procedures. When questioned about his previous work experience, Chip had explained he had been working at the Valley Falls Sugar Bowl and would like to have a job where he could work hard and get in shape for the fall football grind.

"I'm not afraid of work," Chip had added.

Gunner had laughed and winked. "Lay right down beside it and go to sleep, eh? You'd better sign on in the recreation department. Most all the summer softies go for jobs over there. What's the matter with *you?*"

Chip had smiled at that comment but had insisted on an active, outside job. That had settled it. Chip had been assigned to the Yard. He didn't know much about a steel-mill yard, but he was willing to learn if it would keep him in good physical condition. After the four-o'clock whistle had cleared the day shift, Chip had accompanied Gunner Kirk to the Mansfield Steelers Ballpark and had been given a uniform and a locker.

Chip immediately recognized the broad-shouldered athlete dressing next to him. He was thrilled that his locker was right beside Richard Tucker's. Chip was a little overanxious in greeting the famous college star. Tucker chilled the young pitcher's hopes of a quick friendship by his cool appraisal of the slender newcomer. Then he had turned abruptly away with a curt, indifferent hello.

Chip had been surprised and a bit puzzled by Tucker's coolness. Most of the college athletes he had met on his visits to State had been friendly and had made the visiting athletes feel welcome and comfortable. But Duck had shown by his actions that he had no interest in welcoming the new pitcher. Now Tucker was coming to bat, and Chip had a strong desire to strike him out. There would be some measure of satisfaction in showing the snobby college athlete that Chip Hilton could do a little pitching himself. But he ignored the temptation to make himself look good at the expense of Tucker, and his thoughts went back to another bit of advice the Rock had once given him.

"Baseball players, big-league or bush-league, Chip, are slow to accept a player until they get to know him. Get to know what kind of stuff he's made of—whether or not he can take it as well as dish it out. You'll be in for a lot of razzing, baiting, and heckling from the bench, all right, but I guess you can hold your own. You always could!"

So Chip poured straight practice throws across the center of the plate, and Tucker and the rest of the hitters had a lot of fun with their war clubs. Batter after batter hit Chip's offerings freely. But that didn't worry the lanky kid on the mound. The hits and Buster Dillon's continual gibes had little or no effect on Chip Hilton's calm composure. He continued to throw carefully, remembering his high school coach's warning about his arm. As he worked, though, he couldn't resist comparing

THE NEW HURLER

Gunner Kirk's methods to Rockwell's. The "Rock" never asked anyone to pitch, even for batting practice, until he had warmed up thoroughly, until he felt right.

Gunner Kirk had sent Chip out on the hill stone cold. Chip was just beginning to feel loose, but he had made up his mind not to bear down no matter what Kirk or Dillon thought about how well he could or couldn't pitch.

Gunner Kirk and Buster Dillon weren't the only people who were disappointed that afternoon with Chip Hilton's pitching efforts. In the grandstand, directly behind home plate, H. L. Armstrong, president of the Mansfield Steel Company, sat beside his daughter Rachel. But Rachel Margaret Armstrong would have been surprised if anyone had called her by her given name; she was known to her parents, teachers, neighbors, and friends only as Peggy, a special name she shared with her grandmother.

There was little physical resemblance between H. L. Armstrong and his only child. H. L. was tall and heavily built, while Peggy, medium height, was slim and athletic. Although Peggy looked like and, of course, loved her mom, she had more in common with her dad. Each had a keen sports mind and a love for the outdoors and its freedom. During the school year, Peggy attended a private girls' school in a neighboring town. But in the summer, she took a job in her father's plant, working as a receptionist in the recreation department. She enjoyed working for her dad and helping out at the plant. Even more, she loved baseball and was proud of her dad's accomplishments, especially in the Industrial Baseball League.

Anyone wanting to see H. L. and Peggy Armstrong would have known where to find them; everyone knew they'd be at the ballpark after the close of the day's work, watching the Steelers practice. Now they were eyeing the new teenager on the pitcher's mound.

"He has a nice delivery, Dad," Peggy ventured.

H. L. Armstrong squinted his eyes as he concentrated on the tall, gray-eyed, blond youngster. "Yes," he agreed half-aloud, "he's loose, all right. But he doesn't seem to have much on the ball." He shook his head doubtfully and, with a sigh, reluctantly stood up. "Well, I suppose we ought to go home. Right?"

Peggy picked up the copy of the *Mansfield Journal* her father had dropped on the seat beside her. It was folded to the sports page, and a headline caught the girl's eye.

STEELERS PITCHING STAFF STRENGTHENED
All-State Star Reports

William "Chip" Hilton, touted hurler of the state championship Valley Falls nine, will appear in a Steelers uniform for the balance of the summer baseball season. Hilton was the star in Valley Falls High School's successful quest for state honors and will undoubtedly strengthen the Steelers' bid for the city championship.

The Steelers have lost their last five games. Duck Tucker, State's great star and the Steelers' number-one chucker, won his initial start, beating Tri-State 6-2. But since then, he has dropped two in a row to the high-flying Mackin Motors, 4-3 and 6-1.

Manager Kirk has been handicapped thus far because of weak pitching, and the All-State high school star will be welcomed with open arms. Hilton was credited with eleven consecutive victories during the regular season and won his twelfth-straight in the first game of the championship series at University. Kirk said yesterday he would probably start Hilton against the Fitzgerald Painters on Saturday.

It was too bad H. L. Armstrong and Peggy didn't remain in the grandstand a few minutes longer because they—and Gunner Kirk too—might have seen something that would have eased their doubts about the pitcher Coach Henry Rockwell had recommended so highly.

CHAPTER 2

High School Squirt

GOOD CATCHERS are hard to find, chiefly because kids, as a whole, can't see much glamour in the tough work of a catching assignment. Most kids want to pitch. They dream of being another Roger Clemens, Nolan Ryan, Tom Seaver, Bob Gibson, or Jim Palmer. And that's great! But when they don't achieve their ambitions as first-class pitchers, most baseball players then turn to the infield or outfield positions.

But there are certain hardy, courageous athletes who see a future in this toughest of all baseball jobs. And they are wise. They're smart because it's the humble catcher who will probably succeed in the game when the would-be pitcher will fail. Great catchers, like Johnny Bench, are rare. Those catchers who prove themselves are usually good leaders, and because of their importance in handling pitchers, calling the plays, and generally directing team play, they have the most consistent success in organized baseball. Not only is this true of their playing days but also later when it comes to landing coaching and managing jobs.

On the physical side, the only reason Gunner Kirk had failed to qualify as a big-league catcher was because he couldn't throw accurately to second base. Kirk could make the short, hard throws to first and third, earning him his nickname. But it was the long throw—the throw to the keystone sack—that held him back. For some strange reason, Kirk had never been able to master that throw. When he got away a quick throw, the ball was just as likely to end up in the dirt or in center field. When he slowed down his motion and tried to aim the ball, the runner always beat the ball to the bag.

Gunner Kirk still might have been able to make it as a professional player, except he also lacked certain personal qualities that usually characterize the big-leaguer. Kirk just didn't have imagination, perception, intuition, or integrity.

As a manager, Kirk had never learned how to lead and direct men. He lacked the vision to see beyond a player's physical ability. He knew nothing about the hearts and souls of athletes or the psychology of sports. But the long years of catching behind the plate had given Gunner one important asset—keen eyesight. From his position behind the mound, he had noticed H. L. Armstrong and his daughter's arrival at the stadium. And that worried Kirk. He didn't like to have his boss around during workouts.

Gunner Kirk had worked for H. L. Armstrong for the past five years. He had a year-round position in the recreation division of Mansfield Steel, but his chief responsibility was the baseball team. So far, the team had not been too successful, and Kirk had vague, uncomfortable feelings about his employer's opinion of his abilities as a baseball manager.

CLUTCH HITTER

Armstrong's attention to the baseball team this year had seemed to Kirk to be more concentrated than in any previous year. He seemed to be around more often, looking more closely at how the team was progressing. Armstrong had summoned Kirk to his office several times and talked about the possibilities of the team, the personnel problems, and the failure of the employees to give the team solid support. Kirk had tried to explain that most everyone likes a winner and that the Steelers could use a few younger players.

These thoughts were bothering Kirk all through batting practice. His alert eyes caught the movement in the grandstand. Good! He was glad the Old Man had seen the practice after all and had had a chance to grab a look at the new pitcher too. Now maybe Armstrong would see how little he had to work with—a hot-headed, money-crazy pitcher, a bunch of broken-down has-beens, and now this high school wannabe who had nothing but a uniform. Kirk wished, too, that H. L. Armstrong would stop second-guessing every move he made. This ball club hadn't been anywhere—the record proved that—and it wasn't going anywhere either, unless it got some real pitching.

Now, when he noticed that Armstrong and Peggy were getting ready to leave the grandstand, Gunner decided to seize this opportunity and see if he couldn't turn it to his own advantage. Armstrong had seen for himself Chip Hilton's weak pitching, and now Gunner could use that poor performance to make a plea for additional pitching help.

He checked Chip and told Buster Dillon he could climb out of his catching gear and take his practice swings.

"About time," Dillon grumbled. "And about time to quit wastin' the whole evening on a high school squirt who oughta be playin' softball."

HIGH SCHOOL SQUIRT

Kirk caught up with the Armstrongs just outside the park. He had made up his mind to confront H. L. over this pitching situation. For the next fifteen minutes he talked over his predicament with the tall, powerfully built president of the company, while Peggy Armstrong stood by reading a copy of a newspaper, which for some reason seemed to interest her very much.

"Yes, I do appreciate your problem, Kirk," Armstrong said thoughtfully. "It's too bad we couldn't have kept Miller in line and on the squad. I still haven't figured out what went wrong with him."

"He wouldn't take orders, Mr. Armstrong. I know it's hard for a company supervisor to take orders from a worker like me, but there can only be one manager on a baseball field."

"That's right, Kirk. Absolutely right. Still, I was surprised at Miller's attitude. He's been with the company a long time, though, and I guess it's his prerogative if he doesn't want to play. What do you suggest?"

"I don't know, Mr. Armstrong. Looks like we're stuck. The city league rules say we can't bring anyone in after the fourth week in June." Kirk hooked a thumb toward the field. "This new kid just got in under the wire."

Kirk hesitated, shuffled his feet awkwardly, and, then with a quick look at Armstrong's face, pressed on, "Maybe we could—er—scare someone up quick."

Armstrong shook his head sternly. "No, no, nothing like that! We don't need pitchers that badly. So far as that's concerned, we don't even need *baseball* that badly."

"I know, I know, Mr. Armstrong," Kirk reassured hastily. "I wasn't thinkin' of doin' anything outta line."

"What about this new teenager? How does he stand up? Is he going to help us?"

Kirk shook his head doubtfully. "I don't think so. He seems a little bullheaded or maybe it's swellheaded. So far he hasn't shown a thing. How did you come to get him, Mr. Armstrong?"

Armstrong smiled. "That's a long story, Kirk. Goes back forty years or more. I hope he turns out all right. In fact, he's almost *got* to turn out all right. If he doesn't, I'll lose a lot of faith in the baseball acumen of someone I admire very much. Fair enough?"

Kirk nodded his head. He was still in the dark about the new pitcher, still hadn't really found out anything about Armstrong's connection with this Hilton kid, but he sensed that pushing for further details right now would be unwise. Yet, he hadn't solved his pitching problem; five losses in a row wasn't much of a record. He wanted to be sure Armstrong knew why the games were being lost.

"I've tried everything. Fact is, I can't even go to sleep nights, tryin' to figure out a way to get us into the winnin' column. We've just got to get another pitcher or two, Mr. Armstrong."

Armstrong placed a friendly hand on Kirk's arm. "Just as long as you're doing the best you can, Kirk, that's all anyone can ask of you. Why don't you take a look at the personnel department records? Who knows? Maybe we've got an Orel Hershiser right here in the plant! Maybe Peggy can help us."

While Kirk was talking to Armstrong, things were happening back on the field. Duck Tucker had come up to bat again. He rapped the plate and then called out contemptuously, "Let's see some of that schoolboy wonder stuff you've been spreading around, Hilton."

It was several seconds before the words registered with Chip. He couldn't believe his ears. What was Tucker talking about? He lobbed an easy one across the plate, and Tucker pulled it sharply over third base.

"Come on, squirt," he called. "Give me one I can ride."

Chip flushed darkly. This had gone far enough. The slow anger that had been coming to a head all afternoon nearly got the best of him. He clenched his glove and gripped the ball tensely for just a second, and then he relaxed and inhaled the fresh summer air. A grin played about the corners of his mouth. OK. He'd give Tucker one he could ride . . . the balloon blooper!

With the same fluid motion, Chip's arm flashed through, and the balloon ball floated up, then down toward the plate. Tucker checked his swing and then tried to kill the ball. But he missed it by a mile, nearly losing his balance and falling over.

"What a ride," someone shouted, "what a ride! Thanks for the cool breeze!"

Chip barely gave Tucker time to get set before he fired a hard one inside, crowding Duck's letters. Again Tucker's bat fanned the breeze. And again a tantalizing shout greeted the star hurler.

"Give it a ride, slugger. That's riding it, DiMaggio!" By the time Chip had secured another ball, Tucker had moved back in the box as far as he could go, and Chip felt a little glow of exultation warming his face. Good! Now he knew that State's star hurler didn't like the fast ones. Well, he'd give the star a chance to look at one that was really fast.

This time, Chip fired a high, hard one that smoked all the way. Tucker didn't even go for it, but Chip had noticed that with each batting stride, Duck's left foot had stepped in the bucket. That was the tip-off, and Chip threw a wide change-up on his curveball that Tucker missed by a foot.

"You swing like Maris and McGuire, 'cept they hit the ball," heckled an outfielder.

Buster Dillon lumbered up to the third-base side of the plate and pushed Tucker roughly out of the way. "C'mon, c'mon, get outta there! You been swingin' all day! Just ride your bat back to the bench."

Then the brawny receiver banged his heavy bat on the plate.

"OK, sweety," he taunted. "Throw that nothin' ball of yours in here and watch it get lost over the fence!"

While Dillon had been catching, Chip hadn't thrown anything but straight pitches. He hadn't once thrown his fastball or any sort of a curve. He waited until Dillon was all set, and then, with the same easy motion he'd been using to pitch all evening, he took a long stride toward third base and blazed a fast curve, shoulder-high and straight at the mouthy catcher.

Dillon dropped like a shot, surprised at the darting speed of the ball. He landed in the dirt and started a protesting shout. But two feet away, the ball dipped right across the heart of the plate and sped into the netting of the batting cage. Buster's mouth swung open in amazement, and for the first time that day he was speechless. Someone near the dugout laughed, and Dillon cast a vicious look in that direction as he scrambled to his feet in silent fury.

"That's losing it, Buster!" The same tantalizing voice Chip had heard before came booming in from the outfield. "That's losing it!"

Chip glanced out in right field where a stocky guy, who looked a couple of years older than him, was cupping his mouth with glove and hand. "Toss one in to him underhand, Hilton. He's good at pepperball hitting!"

Dillon glared at the figure in right field and bellowed, "In your hat, water boy. Get on your horse for this one!"

HIGH SCHOOL SQUIRT

Chip walked slowly behind the mound and took another ball out of the bag. The brief pause gave Dillon a chance to recover some of his poise, but he wasn't quite so confident when he stepped back into the batter's box. Again Chip took a full windup and this time used his screwball. He aimed for the first-base corner of the plate but, wanting to flash another strike past Dillon, gave a little extra snap to his wrist. The ball shot like a streak of lightning to the inside corner just above Buster's knees. It was a strike in any league.

Dillon never moved. He stood frozen like a statue with his bat on his shoulder. But now there was a sudden intentness in his eyes; he was just beginning to realize the challenge that the long-legged athlete was throwing at him with every pitch.

As Chip turned and waited for one of the fielders to wing in another ball, Buster took advantage of the short pause to dig in and get set. There was no razzing now from the forceful catcher; Dillon was deadly silent. But not his teammates. They couldn't resist an opportunity like this to needle the nasty-tempered catcher.

"Hole in that bat?"

"What's the trouble, Buster? Dust in your eyes?"

"What ya waitin' for, Buster? Darkness?"

"Better hit the dirt, slugger!"

"Hurry up! I've got to work tomorrow!"

Dillon made no reply. He wasn't interested in anything now but his personal duel with this smart-aleck high school squirt. He was concentrating desperately on the slender pitcher out there on the mound. Chip again took a full windup and bent a slow, teasing change-up curve toward the plate. Dillon swung mightily and nearly fell flat on his face, but all his bat met was the evening breeze, again. There was another chorus from the watching players.

CLUTCH HITTER

The blustering catcher was worried now. He rapped the plate with his bat, but there wasn't the same sureness in his actions. Chip waited patiently, conscious now that their little drama was attracting and holding the interest of every player on the field. When Buster was all set, Chip took his slow, easy windup, stepped toward third, and then put everything he had into his fastball. It was a fireball if there ever was one, and Dillon went for it too late. The ball thumped into the screen before Buster was halfway through his swing.

There was a hushed silence and then, from behind Chip out in right field, came the shrill call again of the player who had aggravated Dillon before.

"You can't hit 'em if you can't see 'em, Buster!"

That did it! Buster was smoldering now and blind with rage. He mouthed a curse and threw his bat angrily along the ground toward Chip. The bat slithered crazily along the clay to the right of the mound, narrowly missing the young pitcher's legs.

"What ya tryin' to do?" Dillon shouted. "Dust me off? Look, squirt, you put that ball over the plate, or I'll put a bat alongside your pretty head!"

Chip picked up the bat and carefully tossed it back to the angry catcher. Then, without answering, he turned his back on him and waited for another ball. One of the infielders pegged one in to him, and when Chip turned around, Buster had reached the plate again and had dug in, grimly pulling at his belt, yanking his cap down over his left eye, spitting on his hands, and pounding the plate. But Chip had lost all interest in his duel with Dillon. He went back to straight batting-practice throws, and Buster regained some of his lost composure by meeting five in a row for solid clouts.

Yet, there was an unusual quietness and a mean tightness forming around the belligerent catcher's mouth as he rounded the bases after his last hit. The surly receiver knew as well as everyone else on that field that each and every one of those pitches, which had made him look so foolish, had split the plate, had been perfect strikes. And Chip Hilton and everyone else who had watched the little byplay between the two teammates knew that the new hurler had made an enemy of Buster Dillon.

CHAPTER 3

"Call Me Jake"

STEEL WORKERS are rugged. It seems as though the strength of the metal they work with somehow transfers itself to the workers themselves and gives them some of its toughness. Rough in manner and hardened to the demands of their exhausting labor, they have strong likes and dislikes and little respect for weaklings.

Chip was on the eight-to-four day shift, and the clock registered 7:50 A.M. on his time card when he filed through the plant gate. As he made his way to the Yard office, Chip looked around hoping to see a familiar face. One or two workmen nodded to him, but he didn't recognize them. However, at the Yard office he was successful. One of the outfielders he had seen the evening before at the ballpark greeted Chip with a cheerful, "Hi ya! What are you doing out here in the Yard?"

"Reporting for work! Do you know where I can find Mr. Miller?"

"CALL ME JAKE"

"Jake Miller? Sure! He's in the office over there. You gonna work in the Yard?"

Chip told him he'd specifically asked for a job in the Yard because he wanted to work outdoors. Chip and the friendly outfielder hit it off right from the start, and the two were soon talking in a free and easy way. Chip learned that Bobby Barber knew everyone in the Yard. Chip could tell from the way he talked that the husky, good-looking Barber got a kick out of everything he did and had the ability to infect everybody around him with that same good feeling.

Bobby Barber was just under six feet, and the 190 pounds he carried was solidly packed on his strong frame. His blue eyes seemed to be amused most of the time, and Chip soon found himself laughing with and at Bobby's easygoing approach. Then Chip realized who Barber was. He was the player who had yelled something about Buster Dillon's eyesight the evening before when the grouchy catcher had been at bat. Gunner Kirk hadn't bothered to introduce Chip to the rest of the team, but this was one teammate Chip had liked even before they had actually met.

Chip had wanted a tough job—one to keep him in shape. Well, he had it all right.

There were eighteen or twenty men in Chip's work crew, and their first job was unloading a car of iron castings. Chip jumped into the freight car and enthusiastically began loading the metal hopper. But his zest didn't last long. This was hard, back-breaking work!

Chip quickly learned the best method was to pace himself with the others. The grim-faced men worked steadily; they worked without haste and without wasted motion. There was little conversation, and Chip couldn't help comparing his present surroundings and work with his old job at the Valley Falls Sugar Bowl. But he deliberately forced himself to concentrate on the job in front of him and on the Mansfield Steelers baseball team.

"How's the new pitcher shape up? The high school kid?" called one of the unloading crew to Bobby Barber.

Chip pretended not to hear the conversation. And although Barber lowered his voice, Chip clearly heard his reply.

"He looks good! Sure made Buster Dillon back up in batting practice last night!"

"They tell me he's only a kid, 'bout seventeen—"

"Yeah, but he won eleven straight in the regular season and then won the state title for Valley Falls. Got the outstanding player award. That isn't too bad, is it?"

"Aw, high school pitchers are high school pitchers! They're just kids! Nothing to get all excited about."

"Bob Feller was only a kid when he went to the majors!"

"Yeah, but Bob Fellers don't come along everyday. Especially by way of the Mansfield Steel Company."

"I tell you he's great! You just wait! You'll see!"

"Aw, tell it to Ripley's Believe it or Not! Get back to work!"

Chip didn't look up but kept at his job. His back and arms began to ache, and he couldn't help wishing he'd been a little less adamant about looking for a tough job. He glanced down at his hands. Ugly blisters had already formed on several of his finger tips, and there were red burning marks across his palms. He had forgotten to buy a pair of gloves. That would be the first thing he'd do at lunchtime.

"How's your first day goin'?"

Chip looked up to meet the quizzical eyes of Jake Miller, the Yard boss. Miller was looking at Chip's hands, noting the reddened fingers. He shook his head and smiled.

"You're makin' a big mistake handlin' steel without gloves, kid. You've got good hands, but you won't have them long if you don't cover 'em up. Steel's awfully rough on the skin."

"I know, Mr. Miller, but I didn't have a chance to get a pair this morning. I'll get some at noon."

"That'll be too late. Here, use these!"

Chip thanked the foreman for the gloves and slowly pulled them on his hands. He didn't say anything, but he was thinking that it was already too late.

Miller looked down at his own hands and then rubbed them together. "Yep," he said, "that's where it is in baseball—or in any other game, I guess. In the hands. You're goin' to be stiff tonight, kid. Probably won't feel much like practicing. Rustlin' steel's a tough job!"

Chip nodded ruefully. "It sure is," he agreed. "Guess I'll be in pretty good shape for football by the time this summer is over."

"Yeah, guess you will," Miller drawled. "Yeah, if you stick it out that long. Not many kids can take this kind of work—men either, as far's that's concerned. Most of the ballplayers take the easy jobs. Like Duck Tucker. You don't see him doin' any heavy work. Not Duck! Nope, he spends his time in the recreation department, doin' office work. Hah!" Miller spat contemptuously.

"I like hard work," Chip said quietly. "I'll stick it out, Mr. Miller."

Miller's smile was friendly. "I hope so," he said. "By the way, everyone calls me Jake. Get it?"

It seemed hours before the noon break came. Chip dropped wearily out of the boxcar and found Barber waiting for him.

"Saw you talking to Jake Miller," Bobby said curiously. "What'd he have to say?"

"Oh, he gave me these gloves. Good thing he did!"

"Say anything about baseball?"

"A little. He seems to like baseball."

Barber nodded his head enthusiastically. "He sure does," he agreed. "Guess that's why he gave me a break with the loader. Jake's a good pitcher. He's a little old and most of his fast stuff is gone, but you can't beat a pitcher like Jake Miller when it comes to control and using his head."

Barber looked around cautiously, then lowered his voice. "Miller hates Kirk and Dillon. He was the best pitcher we had next to Tucker last year, but he wouldn't take any flack from Dillon, and they had an argument. Then he and Kirk tangled. Jake's tougher than he looks, let me tell ya. It all ended up with him poking Gunner in the nose and then quitting the team. I'll tell you more about it later. Meet me at the gate at four o'clock. OK?"

The four o'clock shift change found Chip Hilton thoroughly subdued. Every muscle in his body ached. For the first time in his life, Chip wished he could pile into bed in the middle of the afternoon and stay there for a week. But baseball practice and a stronger sense of personal pride wouldn't permit him to show any evidence of weakness. He could take it.

On the way to the ballpark, Barber gave Chip no chance to talk. The exhausted teenager was glad. He was too tired to talk, and listening to Bobby gave him a rest and a chance to find out more about his summer teammates. As he suspected, Barber particularly disliked Kirk and Dillon and made no effort to hide how he felt.

"Not because I never get a chance to play," he told Chip quickly, "but because they're not regular guys. Kirk made Dillon the field captain, and every player on the team hates the guy. Everybody except Tucker. I can't figure out the connection between Duck and Dillon. It sure beats me! I just don't get it."

Chip learned more about Tucker from his talkative new friend.

"He thinks he's a big wheel," Barber said with open disgust. "A big heel is more like it. He acts like he's better than the other men working here and that ticks me off. You'll get to know some of the men here, Chip. They're hard workers and good people. Tucker also hangs around Peggy Armstrong in the recreation building and is supposed to be a personnel guy."

"Who's Peggy Armstrong?"

Bobby whistled softly and rolled his eyes. "Peggy Armstrong," he said with dramatic emphasis, "is *something! And* she's the big boss's daughter!" He suddenly became serious. "She's a really nice girl, though," he added hurriedly. "Everybody likes her. She doesn't pull any high-hat, upper-class stuff at all."

But Barber wasn't to be kept long from his favorite subject, the Steelers baseball team. Chip learned that Lefty Curtis was a former college first baseman, that he hit and threw left-handed and was a real team player. Curtis worked in the engineering department and loved the game.

"You'll like Shorty Welch," Bobby enthused. "He's a real hustler. He and Joe Ferris, the shortstop, make up a deadly double-play combination. You'll like both those guys, Chip."

Joe Ferris, the shortstop, Shorty Welch, the second baseman, and Don Catolono, the third baseman, all worked in the timekeeping department.

"Those three guys hang around together all the time." Bobby laughed. "They eat and sleep baseball."

CLUTCH HITTER

Chip looked sideways at his companion. "You don't give it much rest either, do you?"

Barber shook his head. "I love baseball. I wish I could play baseball every day of my life.

"The outfield is pretty well set," he continued. "Cooper, in left, Murphy in center, and Pete 'the Arm' Armeda in right, make up the regular outfield. Kirk never shifts the players of his lineup on account of left-hand or right-hand pitching we face. Guess that's the reason I never get a chance to play. All those guys are right-handers at the plate. Lefty Curtis and I are the only lefty hitters on the team. How do you hit, right or left?"

Chip hesitated. He didn't want to tell Barber he was a switch hitter. It seemed too much like bragging. "I like to hit left-handed," he said slowly. "What about the pitching?"

"Besides you and Tucker, we've only got one other pitcher, Softy Simmons. But he's not really a pitcher. Fact is, he isn't a ballplayer at all." Barber sighed resignedly. "But Kirk likes him and that's the reason he's in uniform."

Barber didn't stop with the players. He talked in detail about the league and particularly about the rivalry between the Mansfield Steelers and the Mackin Motors.

"Armstrong, our boss, and old man Mackin are the big players in this town. And they're always trying to outdo each other in one thing or another. It doesn't matter how many games we lose if we can only beat the Mackins. But it doesn't look like we're gonna do it this year. They've already beat us twice—bad!"

Practice that day was a repetition of the first day. Chip was stiff and sore, and his hands were a mass of blisters, but he said nothing when Kirk ordered him out to the mound for batting practice. Chip's arm muscles were tired from the unusual lifting and straining so he again threw straight batting-practice pitches. The hit-

"CALL ME JAKE"

ters liked it and pounded the ball all over the field. After fielding practice, Kirk sent the squad trotting around the field. Then the manager ordered them to the showers. As Chip passed the dugout, Kirk stopped him.

"What's wrong with your arm, Hilton? You haven't shown a thing!"

Chip held down his impulse to reply angrily. He also figured it wouldn't do him any good to try to reason with this man. After a short pause, he replied in an even voice, "There's nothing wrong with my arm, Mr. Kirk. I'm just a little stiff after today's work and—"

"A big stiff's more like it!" Buster Dillon's rasping voice interrupted. "Biggest stiff I ever saw in a baseball uniform!"

Chip's jaw clenched, but he never shifted his eyes from Gunner Kirk's face. He ignored Dillon completely.

Kirk studied Chip thoughtfully. "What was the idea of takin' a job in the Yard?" he queried. "Why didn't you grab one of those soft summer recreation jobs? You're only gonna be here for a couple of months. Why didn't you play it smart? Why work your head off when you don't have to?"

"I . . . I wanted to get toughened up for football, Mr. Kirk."

"Look, Hilton, you weren't brought up here for football. This is a baseball team in case you didn't notice."

Kirk checked himself and glared after the players who were disappearing under the grandstand. Then he continued sarcastically, "At least it's s'posed to be a baseball team. Now with you here, I don't know how it's gonna end up. We'll probably be usin' the T-formation instead of an infield shift—"

"And end up playin' in the American Legion Junior Tournament," Dillon interrupted. He glowered at Chip and then snarled contemptuously. "You oughta go good in *that* league, squirt."

"My name is Chip, Mr. Dillon."

"Chump would be closer to it."

"Look, Mr. Dillon—"

"Don't 'mister' me," Dillon growled. "School's out! You're in the workin' world now, squirt! Be yourself!"

Kirk turned on Dillon and gestured for silence. "That's enough, Buster," he said shortly. "I'll handle this." He turned to Chip. "Look, Hilton, you're s'posed to be a ballplayer. Don't be giving me any alibis about bein' tired or stiff. I don't want talk! I want pitching! Understand?"

Chip's thin lips were set in a straight line, and his eyes narrowed dangerously. He said nothing but merely nodded. Kirk's hard eyes bored into Chip's and held them, but he realized there was no surrender there, and it was the manager who shifted his glance. He waved toward the grandstand. "That's all, Hilton," he said shortly.

Chip turned without a word, and the two men watched the long, quick strides of the angry athlete carry him to the gate by the grandstand and out of sight.

While Kirk and Dillon had been talking, something had flashed through Chip's mind—flashed through with a burning memory. Long ago, when "Big Chip" Hilton had been teaching his son to box and to stand up for his rights, he had said, "If it ever comes to a showdown with two fellows, Chipper, choose the biggest one as your target and then give it to him, but hard! But be sure you've taken as much as you can and be sure you're right."

For one desperate second, Chip Hilton had come close to giving it to Buster Dillon, but hard. But he hadn't taken as much as he could, not yet.

CHAPTER 4

The Boss's Daughter

BOBBY BARBER expertly braked the loader and dropped lightly to the ground before the siren ended its noon wail. Then he sprinted over to Chip. "Come on," he urged with a broad smile. "We're gonna eat in style today. I feel in the mood for some soft, relaxing music and air conditioning with my lunch! We'll eat in the company cafeteria! The food isn't all that good, but I want you to see Peggy Armstrong. Wait till you see her! She eats there every day."

Like most of the Yard workers, Chip brought his lunch to work. He liked that too. Not only because his landlady, Mrs. Pecora, was a good cook and jammed his lunch box with tasty food, but because he could drop down wherever he was on the job and get all the rest he could without wasting any time.

"But I brought my lunch with me," Chip protested.

"So what! I'll help you eat that this afternoon."

"Yeah, but I can't go to the cafeteria looking like this! I'm a mess. Look at me!"

CLUTCH HITTER

Chip was a mess all right. His face was grimy and streaked where rivulets of sweat had run down from underneath his blond hair, and the overalls he had bought Monday afternoon looked as though they had already been worn for months. But Bobby Barber was not about to be denied. He wasn't taking no from Chip Hilton. He'd taken Chip on as his personal responsibility and that was that. So despite Chip's protests, Bobby hurried him in and out of the washroom and across the Yard to H. L. Armstrong's favorite project, the recreation building.

Barber had described the bowling alleys, pool tables, basketball court, small library, and staff meeting rooms, but this was Chip's first visit to the building. Now he could understand Barber's enthusiasm. Everything was just as Bobby had described it—shiny, well-equipped, and spotlessly clean—just the opposite of the Yard.

The pair entered the cafeteria. Chip felt self-conscious and ill at ease as he picked up a tray and utensils and fell in line behind Barber. As he moved along the counter, selecting his lunch from the plates filled with sandwiches, salads, and hot entrees, he felt his face reddening. Why had he let Barber talk him into this? He sure was out of place. No one in the big room, except Bobby and himself, was wearing Yard work clothes.

Barber suddenly nudged Chip's arm. "Look," he whispered, "there she is! She's right behind you!"

Chip turned quickly. His elbow hit something hard. And that something was Peggy Armstrong's tray. Soup, coffee, plates, silverware, and food went flying up into the air and then came crashing down to the floor. Chip couldn't believe it! He nearly dropped his own tray. He stood there staring for an instant and then quickly placed his tray on the serving counter and began to pick up the scattered knives, forks, spoons, and broken pieces of plates.

THE BOSS'S DAUGHTER

Chip was so embarrassed he didn't even think to apologize. But as he bent over, he caught a fleeting glimpse of big, brown startled eyes, framed in the clear, tanned complexion of one of the most attractive faces he had ever seen.

Peggy Armstrong's "Oh!" was followed by the loud laughter of her lunch companion. Chip would have known that laugh and the voice that followed it anywhere.

"You do that as though you've had experience, Hilton. What do you know! A gentleman steel hustler!"

Chip seethed inside, but he ignored Tucker completely. Barber was frantically mopping up the mess from the floor. When he heard Tucker's mocking words, he stood up and gestured as if to throw the wet napkins in Tucker's face. But Chip was between Bobby and Tucker now, facing Peggy Armstrong.

"I'm sorry," Chip managed. "I'm really sorry. I'll get you another tray and pay for the damage."

"It's OK. That's not necessary," Peggy Armstrong assured him. "It was an accident. It's happened before. Don't worry about it!"

But Tucker couldn't resist this opportunity. "They teach you all that grace in high school, Hilton?" Then he laughed boisterously. But his face lost its smirk when Peggy Armstrong placed a hand on Chip's arm and spoke to him quietly and earnestly.

"I've changed my mind. If you still mean it, I *will* let you buy my lunch. I'm sure Mr. Tucker here is smart enough to understand why a lady prefers to eat her lunch in the company of a gentleman."

Bobby nearly lost it! He choked with triumph for Chip. He aimed a jubilant glance in Tucker's direction and hurried away to get a clean tray.

"My name is Rachel Armstrong," Peggy said with the whitest smile Chip had ever seen. "Actually, it's Rachel

Margaret Armstrong, but fortunately everyone calls me Peggy." That smile again. "And since I already know who you are, we won't have to wait for Bobby to introduce us." She laughed softly. "Not that he'd ever think of it! About all he ever thinks about is baseball, baseball, baseball!"

Chip and Peggy moved out of the serving line while Duck Tucker continued on alone. But there was a sneer on his face and a hard light in his eyes as he eyed Chip for an instant and then swaggered along the line.

Despite Peggy's graciousness, Chip felt completely ridiculous. Because of the typical confusion and clatter of the cafeteria line, only a few employees had seen the accident. Even those who had seen Chip knocking Peggy's tray in the air had quickly turned away and concentrated on their lunchtime conversations and eating before they headed back to their offices. But no one could have told that to Chip Hilton. He hadn't looked around, but he was sure he must be the focus of everyone's eyes. He glanced at Peggy Armstrong and half-smiled. Then he was struck by a horrible thought. He had only a five-dollar bill in his pocket!

Chip's brain was in a turmoil. How much had he already spent? Was it two dollars and forty cents, or was it two dollars and sixty cents? Was it even more? He groaned inwardly. Why had he offered to pay for Peggy's lunch? Why had he said anything at all? He wished he had stayed in the Yard for lunch.

Then he had a flash of hope, and he looked at Peggy's trim figure in one fleeting glance. She wasn't very big. Maybe she didn't eat much, wouldn't be very hungry.

But Peggy Armstrong was an active girl. Chip didn't know that the slender girl was a vigorous athlete: Mansfield's junior tennis champion, a fine golfer, and an outstanding swimmer.

So, as Chip followed Peggy Armstrong along with the

trays of food and watched her add item after item to an already substantial lunch, he felt little beads of moisture gathering on his forehead, and he was lost in a maze of mathematical calculations. When he reached the cashier at the end of the counter, Chip's financial worries mounted. Before the cashier had finished ringing up the two trays, Chip had figured the total. He was short twenty-five cents. Oh, for one little quarter!

He looked around for Bobby. But he'd already boldly led the way to a table right in the center of the room, and Peggy Armstrong had followed. Chip fumbled in his overalls and produced a rumpled five-dollar bill. He risked a worried glance at the cashier, but she was busy looking at the clock and impatiently tapping the counter with her pencil. Chip renewed his frenzied search of his pockets, hoping for a miracle and desperately feeling for a hidden quarter.

"What's the matter, big spender?" drawled a loud voice. "Forget your milk money or your gold credit cards? Now you know why they tell ya to never leave home without them!" Tucker was seated at a table not ten feet away.

Chip turned around and met Tucker's sarcastic smile. For one second Chip considered dashing the tray into that sneering face, but reason kicked in and he turned back to the cashier.

"I guess I'll have to owe you the twenty-five cents," he said anxiously, handing the cashier the five-dollar bill. "Will it be all right if I bring it in tomorrow?"

Chip had never seen a warmer, wider smile. "Of course, young man," the cashier said simply, smiling again. "Of course it will be all right!"

Tucker's loud laugh followed Chip almost to the table where Peggy and Barber waited.

"What's that creep up to now?" Bobby muttered darkly.

Chip shrugged. "Nothing important. Nothing that can't be taken care of a little later on."

The half hour that followed was one of the shortest in Chip Hilton's life, but during it he learned a lot about H. L. Armstrong and his daughter. As Coach Rockwell had told Chip, the sports-minded president of the Mansfield Steel Company had started from entry level as a Yard laborer forty years ago. But success had not changed H. L. Armstrong. He still loved sports and remembered his early struggles to get ahead. That was the big reason for the profit-sharing and bonus plans in effect at the plant and for the splendid recreation building and programs. H. L. wanted happy employees.

Peggy Armstrong was definitely her father's daughter. The two were almost inseparable during the summer months. Peggy attended a private girls' school, but she admitted to Chip and Bobby that she'd rather go to the local high school so she could live at home. But her mom wanted her to attend the school she herself had graduated from and so Peggy spent the school year at Heatherton.

"This conversation is all one-sided," Peggy said abruptly. "Let's talk about you, Chip, and—"

"And a little about baseball," Bobby suggested hopefully.

Peggy ignored the interruption and eyed Chip curiously. "How do you like the Yard?" she asked.

"Fine, except that—"

"Except what?"

"Nothing much. The work is all right and everything, but the men don't seem very friendly—"

Bobby had been waiting for an opportunity to get into this conversation and this was it. "Oh, they'll warm up," he said, nodding his head. "It's just that right now you're getting the *treatment*. A light going-over! They give that silence stuff to all the new guys. It's kind of a testing period until they see what sort of a guy you are. Besides, they want to make sure you're gonna stick it out."

"Oh, that's right," Peggy said, laughing. "It's something like the fun they have with the Yard Court—"

Bobby nodded. "Yep, but sometimes the treatment is serious too. After a guy's been on the job for a while and proved he's all right, they cut it out. But if somebody gets out of line with his work, or does something the crew doesn't like, he *really* gets it. Then it isn't any fun. They've run a lot of guys out of the Yard that way."

Chip smiled. "I hope they don't run me out," he said.

"Don't worry about *that*," his new friend said, laughing. "Nobody's gonna run the Steelers' number-one pitcher out." Bobby's mood changed. "Come on, you two, let's talk a little about baseball, please! Ask me a question! After all, this fine dining experience was my idea."

"Well," Chip began, "I'd like to know a little more about this National Amateur Baseball setup. All I know now is that Coach Rockwell said it was all right for me to play because it's amateur baseball and won't affect my eligibility in high school or college."

"He's right, Chip," Bobby interrupted. "Lots of high school and college athletes—guys and girls—play in the association all over the country."

"That's true, Chip." Peggy Armstrong blushed and then paused. "Do you mind if I call you Chip?"

Chip swallowed audibly. "Er . . . no . . . of course not. I'd like it!"

"Chip's team won the state championship this year!" Barber announced. "Chip won twelve straight games!"

Peggy Armstrong smiled knowingly. "I know all about it," she said. "Dad's been talking about nothing else ever since he got a letter from Chip's coach about a month ago. His name's Rockwell, isn't it, Chip?"

Before Chip could reply, Bobby was back with, "Chip'll win the city championship for us this year! You just wait and see!"

Peggy laughed. "He'd better hurry up!" she said mockingly. "The Steelers right now seem to be monopolizing the cellar."

"You know that doesn't mean anything," Bobby said, brushing the statement off with a wave of his hand. "Nothing at all. The Mackins have the only classy team in the league, the only team we have to worry about. Wait a couple of weeks. Wait until Chip gets rolling."

Chip protested. "Wait a minute, Bobby," he cautioned. "You've never even seen me pitch."

"No? Well, I know I saw enough the night before last when you blazed 'em by Tucker and Dillon."

Smiling, Barber reached across the table and tapped Chip on the chest. "Look, big boy, you ain't kiddin' me. I know a real pitcher when I see one. And I know something those other players out on that field don't know! I know that a guy by the name of William 'Chip' Hilton hasn't opened up yet, and when he does—"

Chip quickly realized there was no way he was going to win this exchange, and he changed the subject. "I'd like to know more about the association," he said.

Peggy explained that in the recreation office she had a copy of the constitution and the bylaws, which he could have if he would drop by after work, sometime soon.

Chip wasn't particularly interested in the constitution and bylaws of the National Amateur Baseball Association, but he said he would like to take a copy home to Coach Rockwell. And he would be glad to stop by Peggy Armstrong's office after work to pick up the little book. All afternoon he wondered if today after work would be too soon.

CHAPTER 5

Yard Court

TWELVE SMELTERS! Chip had heard of a smelt. He knew that was a small fish resembling a trout, but a smelter was something new. It sounded familiar, but it smacked of a joke too—like the time Soapy Smith had sent little Paddy Jackson, the Valley Falls High School mascot, for a "diamond cutter."

But Bert Long's face was dead serious, and Chip took the Yard pass and started for the toolroom. On the way, he glanced at the requisition slip again. Twelve smelters . . .

Bert Long was Chip's foreman. The grim-faced boss of the roustabouts, the men who did all the heavy lifting jobs of the Yard, was all business. He was a no-nonsense man who rarely smiled. But he was popular with his men. His popularity with the workers was evident by the good spirit they all showed when they pitched in and followed his orders.

At the toolroom window, Chip laid the requisition sheet on the steel surface and watched the attendant warily.

"*Twelve* smelters? What's the matter with that guy? You sure he told you to come to the Yard toolroom? You musta heard wrong! We ain't got no smelters. Never had no smelters. There ain't that many in the whole mill. You try the main mill."

Chip tried the main mill and struck pay dirt with the first foreman he met. The man smiled as he studied Chip's suspicious expression.

"We don't have twelve smelters to spare," he said seriously. "You go back and tell Bert Long we've only got five and we can't spare 'em. OK?"

Chip started to walk away.

"Hey, where you going?"

Chip halted his brisk stride to meet Jake Miller's sharp question.

"Back to Mr. Long," Chip said, extending the requisition slip and his pass.

Miller studied the piece of paper intently. "Have you had any luck?" he asked.

"Yes, sir. Yes, I have. They didn't have any smelters at the toolroom, but there's five at the main mill. The foreman there though—Pete Max—"

Miller interrupted. "It's pronounced Maxomovich," he said with a wide grin.

"Well, Pete Maxomovich said he couldn't spare them."

Miller glanced at his watch. "We'll see about that," he said angrily. "*You* wait right here!"

Chip waited, conscious of the curious looks of several men who passed. He glanced anxiously at the big clock mounted on the wall next to the flagpole. At five minutes of twelve, Jake Miller, a broad smile on his face, came hurrying along, followed by seven of the largest, toughest-looking men Chip had ever seen.

"Here's seven smelters, Hilton," Miller said, his eyes twinkling with mischief. "You hurry them right over to Bert Long." He gestured to a massive steelworker who was frowning. "This is Ralph Iron. We all call him Pig Iron. He's in charge. Pig Iron, this is Chip Hilton."

The big smelter's hamlike paw nearly crushed Chip's hand. He tried to meet Pig Iron's pressure by gripping with his own hand, but all he accomplished was bringing a quick smile to the corner of the giant's hard mouth.

"Glad to meet you, Chippy," Pig Iron said. "Let's go!"

Bert Long's expectant eyes clouded when he looked from Chip to his companions. He tried a brief smile toward the leader, but Pig Iron's face was set in an angry expression.

"Sorry I couldn't get back sooner, Mr. Long," Chip said hastily, "but I had to go to the main mill and they had only seven—"

"Yeah, that's right," Pig Iron growled. "Now, what's the idea of chasin' us all the way up here? What d'ya got lined up that's needin' *our* attention?"

Bert Long was speechless. What had started out as a joke on the kid, Chip Hilton, had boomeranged—on him! Behind him, the Yard gang winked at each other and exchanged knowing smiles. This was going to be good. Long flashed a quick, questioning look at Chip. But he learned nothing there because Chip was clueless himself.

"Why, you see, Pig Iron," Bert began, "er, well—"

"Well, what?" a surly voice from the smelting crew demanded. "Quit stallin'. You ordered smelters, didn't you?"

"Yes, but—"

Pig Iron pushed his way forward and pointed a huge finger at Long. "No buts! C'mon, c'mon, what you want us to do? We gotta get back to our work."

"But it was all just a joke."

Pig Iron pressed still closer, his huge body completely overshadowing Long. "You mean you pulled a joke on us?"

"No! Not on you men, but—"

"A joke, eh? Well, we don't like jokes, see?"

"Let's throw him in the trough!" someone standing behind Pig Iron rasped.

But Pig Iron wasn't through with Long yet. He suddenly shot a huge hand and forearm forward and grasped Long roughly by the shoulder. Then he playfully shook the foreman from side to side. "Who's the joke on if it ain't on us? Huh? Hear that siren? That's twelve o'clock! We walked all the way up here on our own time. What's the joke?"

"It's not on you, Pig Iron," Long protested. "I was just pulling a joke on the new kid."

"Yeah? Well, you counted us in, didn't you? We don't like it an' I think we got a grievance. What you say, men? Yard Court?"

The suggestion met with an immediate roar of approval. Long struggled, but he didn't have a chance of eluding Pig Iron's viselike grip, and he was forced along ahead of the procession.

"Yard Court!" a voice shouted. "Yard Court!"

The shout was taken up by others and spread all over the Yard. Ahead of the group, Chip could hear others shouting the words and soon the phrase echoed from all parts of the Yard.

The parade grew in numbers with almost every step, and soon several hundred workers were pushing and cheering the group forward. Chip was carried along with the crowd, still wondering what was happening.

"In the trough!"

"Teach him to swim!"

YARD COURT

"Yard Court!"

Long was lifted to a wooden loading platform near one of the water troughs. The smelters gathered immediately below him while Pig Iron scrambled up beside the chagrined Yard boss.

"Where's the judge?" someone shouted. "Where's Big Nose?"

A fat man with the biggest, reddest nose Chip had ever seen came pushing his way through the crowd. "Here I am," he shouted. "What's the charge?"

"Holdin' up production. Wastin' time!" Pig Iron shouted.

Big Nose managed to haul his huge bulk up on the platform beside Long and Pig Iron. "Court's in session!" he shouted. "Who's for the defendant?"

"I am!" A voice familiar to Chip shouted. "I'll defend the defendant!"

The crowd quieted as Jake Miller pushed forward and climbed up on the other side of Big Nose. Pig Iron told the eager crowd that Bert Long had ordered smelters for the Yard. Everyone knew there wasn't anything a smelter or any member of a smelter crew could do in the Yard. Seven of them had been humiliated by this, by this—

Pig Iron searched for a word and then ended with, "this junk peddler! On our *own* time, too," he added in an aggrieved voice. "On our *own* time! That's what hurts *most!* We rest our case on *that!*"

Big Nose called for the defense. Jake Miller faced Pig Iron and shook his fist at him. "So, it's humiliated you are," he cried. "Humiliated? Why you should be proud that we even permit you dainty, hothouse flowers out here in our beautiful Yard. Humiliated! Hah!" He gestured toward Pig Iron with disgust and turned to Big Nose.

"I move the defendant be released inasmuch as nothing was lost. Nothing was lost because Pig Iron and the rest of his ironheads were on their *own* time and even you, Big Nose, know a smelter's time is worthless! Especially when he's on his own time."

"Any rebuttal?" Big Nose demanded.

"Yes!" bellowed Pig Iron. "Plenty! *I* move that the defendant and the defendant's mouthpiece *both* be found guilty! Because *Jake Miller's* the one who told us to report to Long. I move not that the defendant be *released*— *but* that the defendant and his accomplice get the treatment. The defendant and Miller *both* get doused!"

"He's right!"

"We want justice!"

"Douse 'em both!"

Big Nose raised both arms and shouted for silence. When quiet was restored, he asked for the usual jury finding.

"For the prosecution!" he shouted.

A tremendous roar greeted the question. "Guilty!" rang from every corner of the Yard.

"For the defense?"

It was incredible. Chip couldn't believe it. He could have heard a whisper. There wasn't a sound. Then Big Nose smiled victoriously and deeply bellowed, "Guilty!"

Immediately there was a response that could be compared only to the roar of a baseball crowd when a clutch hit sails out of the park or to the tumult that follows a desperate, last-second victory field goal to break a tie score or to the eruption accompanying a perfect three-pointer as it arches through the air turning a two-point defeat into a resounding basketball win.

Miller and Long were pulled off the platform and unceremoniously plunged in the trough. The spectators' deafening roar of approval accompanied the huge splash, and then the two water-soaked Yard men were pushed back up on the platform. Both were laughing in spite of their impromptu immersion. As both men dried their faces and hands, the crowd razzed them unmercifully.

Miller raised his hand. "It was a just decision," he shouted laughingly. "A just decision, even though it's a little early for my Saturday night bath."

That afternoon Miller and Long caught it from all sides, and for the first time Chip felt like one of the Yard workers. Especially when the now dry Bert Long winked at Chip and said cheerfully, "Some fun, eh, kid?"

That evening after work, Gunner Kirk sent Chip to the hill again. But this time, Buster Dillon was relieved of the catching assignment, and the batting cage was rolled into place behind the plate.

And, as on the three previous days, Chip threw controlled strikes across the plate, and the hitters again teed off with glee.

Gunner Kirk had been looking at pitchers for thirty years. He knew what to look for when it came to sizing up a hurler, but this squirt had him puzzled. The tall, long-armed kid was loose and had the smooth, easy delivery that denotes speed. But so far, all Chip Hilton had shown the Steelers manager was good batting-practice control.

Kirk couldn't figure it out. Most high school pitchers he'd met had been showoffs, eager to strut their stuff, sensitive to criticism, and quick to respond to a little baiting and badgering. But this kid was different. Nothing seemed to get under his skin, not even Buster Dillon's riding. And that was something! Kirk often found it difficult himself to bear up under the garrulous catcher's sarcastic gibes.

CLUTCH HITTER

After practice, Kirk joined Dillon near the dugout, and, as usual, the two collaborators reviewed the day's workout.

"Don't look like the Hilton kid will help us much, does it?" Kirk asked morosely.

Dillon rolled his chewing tobacco over to the other cheek before answering. "Naw," he growled, "it don't. But I wouldn't be too sure." He shook his head in a puzzled manner and then continued. "I don't get it. Just don't get it."

"Get what?"

"Don't get what Old Man Armstrong's got in mind. He's been cryin' about winnin' the championship and still he doesn't get us any pitchers."

"I agree with that, but I guess he's trying. He got Hilton."

Dillon spat in disgust. "Hilton! Why didn't he get a couple of experienced pitchers? Someone like Bill Haley. Bill can still throw and besides he needs the money."

"But Haley's played pro ball for years."

"So what?"

"You know what! A pro can't play amateur ball! That's what!"

"Aw, nobody checks up on guys like Haley or on things like that."

Kirk was annoyed, but he spoke patiently as though he were explaining a simple problem to a child. "Look, Buster, this National Amateur Baseball Association is different. It's organized and it's pure amateur."

"What if Bill changed his name? What's wrong with that?"

"Nothin'! Nothin', except he couldn't get away with it. The employment department would check his references, or someone would recognize him. No. We couldn't get to first base with that sort of a deal. Besides, our names *would* be mud if we got mixed up with guys like Haley."

YARD COURT

"I can't see as it's any different than our Sunday business deals. We ain't been havin' any trouble gettin' away with that."

Kirk's voice was sharp. "But it *is* different," he said impatiently. "The semipro teams aren't organized and nobody cares who you are or where you're from. But the association's an amateur outfit. Every player's checked, and a company can't pay players for playin' ball, and if a team uses a pro, they lose their membership. Besides, Old Man Armstrong would blow his top if we tried to pull a stunt like that. He wants us to win, but if we did anything like that, why, we'd *all* lose our jobs!"

There was a sudden silence now between the two cronies. Kirk was the leader in the personal business of this combination, and sometimes their actions got a bit beyond his control. Right now he was worried about Dillon's reference to their Sunday business. He was thinking that he had been extremely foolish to risk the loss of a good job just to earn a few extra dollars each week. Especially when Dillon and Tucker got the biggest share of the money. After a short, tense silence, Kirk resumed the conversation.

"Speakin' of the Sunday deal, Buster, I *am* worried about it. The cut I'm gettin' isn't enough to risk losin' my job over."

"If you wasn't such a chump, you'd take a bigger cut away from Tucker. You better be gettin' someone else lined up anyway. Duck's lookin' worse every time he pitches."

"I been thinkin' about that," Kirk said thoughtfully. "I'd been hopin'—"

"Yeah, I know," Dillon interrupted. "You was hopin' this Hilton kid would work in. Duck never works hard for our Saturday games. He likes that extra fifty he gets when he wins in the other league on Sunday."

"We've got to do somethin' this week. We play a tough outfit at Glendale next Sunday, and Duck won't be any good Saturday. It looks like it'll have to be Softy again."

Dillon shifted his feet and shook his head stubbornly. "Look, Gunner," he said slowly, "we gotta win a coupla games for Armstrong, and we ain't gonna do it with Softy. The guy's no ballplayer and you know it! He couldn't make a Little League team!"

Kirk nodded his agreement. "I know, Buster, I know that. But who else is there? If that guy Miller hadn't been such a hardhead, we'd a been all right."

"Why don't you start the squirt?" Dillon asked.

"I've been thinkin' about that," Kirk said thoughtfully. "You know there's somethin' wrong with that kid. He can't be as bad as he's looked. He's got too good a reputation." Kirk shook his head decisively. "OK, maybe I'll start him Saturday. Might as well find out right away whether he's gonna help us."

"What about Duck?" Dillon asked. "We gotta quit pitchin' him on Saturdays altogether, if we're gonna use him Sundays for that easy money. An' we gotta win a couple of games for Armstrong pretty soon or he's gonna start wondering."

Kirk's face was grim. "I know," he said, "I know. Tucker don't even pretend anymore when he's in a Steelers game. The Old Man is bound to see what's plain as the nose on his face. And another thing, Duck's gettin' a little hard to handle. You'd a thought I was askin' him for a thousand bucks instead of just askin' him to throw a few for hittin' practice this afternoon."

Dillon nodded. "Yeah," he said understandingly, "I noticed that. Guess most of the other guys heard his squawk too." He paused and then continued significantly, "Maybe I oughta rough him up a bit."

YARD COURT

"No, there's a better way," Kirk said harshly. "I'll just remind him he's got another year to play up there at the university. And then I'll sorta suggest that his coach and the university people might not like it if they knew he was pitchin' for a little money every Sunday."

CHAPTER 6

"Pretty Boy"

GRANDSTAND LOCKER rooms in most ballparks are notoriously barren and lackluster. The locker room under the grandstand of the Mansfield Steelers home field didn't look much different from others he'd seen, except it was the coldest dressing room Chip Hilton had ever felt. It wasn't H. L. Armstrong's fault. It wasn't the temperature. It wasn't the dressing area and shower facilities either. The locker room contained the best materials and equipment. No, nothing was physically wrong with the place. What was strange was what was missing. Chip could feel the absolute absence of team warmth and enthusiasm; the players shared no togetherness, no spirit, no friendliness.

Locker room spirit is an intangible entity that says a lot about what sort of a squad or team is housed within those four walls. Even when they're losing, most teams can shake off depression in their own dressing rooms. Athletes can pull together as a team in a locker room and pump themselves up for future wins. But this team had no life even after a good session of warm-up practice. Chip knew the Steelers had lost five in a row, but the race had just begun; six weeks of the campaign still remained. There was no reason for the team to feel this low because of a bad start. Even championship professional teams often started slowly. It wasn't just the defeats. It was something else. Something was taking all the fun out of the game for the Steelers—even for those who loved playing the game. There was an absolute lack of the usual practice and locker room gibes, horseplay, taunts, pepper, and laughter. The place was cold.

Chip stretched his back muscles as far as they would go as he bent to lace his baseball cleats. When he had tied them carefully, he straightened up and leaned back against the locker, letting his thoughts drift back to Valley Falls and his Big Reds pals. If only Soapy and Biggie and Speed and Taps were here . . . . The Big Reds' dressing rooms had never been like this, not even in the football days of the bitter feud with Fats Ohlsen.

There wasn't a sound in the room, and Chip suddenly experienced overwhelming homesickness. Here it was only the first week in July, a short week after he and all the guys had won the state high school championship. But all that seemed years ago. He missed the camaraderie of his home team, yet he'd have to stick it out here until September. He couldn't turn back now; he couldn't quit.

This was Friday, Chip's fifth day with the team and his fourth on the job with the Yard crew. Every muscle in his body ached. He absent-mindedly kneaded the muscles of his right forearm and wished Pop Brown was around to give him a rubdown.

The Yard workers had been slow to accept Chip, even though he had earned their grudging respect by doing his full share of the killing work. Chip knew the men were all watching him, expecting him to give in. But that very challenge added strength to Chip's desire to prove he was no quitter and provided the reason why he always did more than his share of the work assigned to his crew.

Even the evenings at the baseball park hadn't been pleasant. Tucker was openly antagonistic. Buster Dillon continued to direct his loud abuse Chip's way and had worn Chip's nerves to a thin edge. With the exception of Barber, the other players hadn't said much to him. Some had barely looked at him. But Chip had expected that. He felt sure they were waiting to find out just what kind of ballplayer he was. They wanted to find out whether he could really pitch or was just another high school flash.

He glanced down at the little piece of tape he had wound around his right forefinger. That finger was as sore as a boil, but he hadn't let on. He had pitched all week without a murmur. Lonely as he was, it was a pleasure to sit here alone in the dressing room and relax for a minute or two after the others had gone out on the field. Chip closed his eyes for a moment, then he sighed, got slowly to his feet, and started for the field. As he neared the door, he saw the schedule card on the bulletin board and stopped to read it. The card was fingered and covered with dust and grime, but the record was out there in the open for everyone to see. Someone had written in the scores of the games and the names of the pitchers. Chip noted Tucker's record. The star had won his first game and lost the next two, both to Mackin Motors. Simmons had been badly beaten all three times he had worked.

MANSFIELD STEEL COMPANY
Baseball Schedule

Wed.	JUNE 8	TRI-STATE	CITY STADIUM	6-2 Tucker
Sat.	JUNE 11	FITZGERALD	NORTH PARK	4-13 Simmons
Wed.	JUNE 15	MACKIN	CITY STADIUM	3-4 Tucker
Sat.	JUNE 18	RITTER	HOME	3-19 Simmons
Wed.	JUNE 22	MACKIN	HOME	1-6 Tucker
Sat.	JUNE 25	TRI-STATE	HOME	2-14 Simmons
Sat.	JULY 2	FITZGERALD	HOME	
Mon.	JULY 4	RITTER	RITTER FIELD	
Wed.	JULY 6	MACKIN	CITY STADIUM	
Sat.	JULY 9	TRI-STATE	CITY STADIUM	
Wed.	JULY 13	FITZGERALD	NORTH PARK	
Sat.	JULY 16	RITTER	HOME	
Wed.	JULY 20	MACKIN	HOME	
Sat.	JULY 23	TRI-STATE	HOME	
Wed.	JULY 27	FITZGERALD	HOME	
Sat.	JULY 30	MACKIN	CITY STADIUM	
Sat.	AUG 6	TRI-STATE	CITY STADIUM	
Sat.	AUG 13	FITZGERALD	NORTH PARK	
Sat.	AUG 20	RITTER	RITTER FIELD	

June 25 brought a little smile to his lips. He'd remember that date for a long while, all right. That was the day he had relieved Nick Trullo with two down in the eighth—for one out! The out that had meant the state championship for Valley Falls. And he guessed he'd remember that third strike about as long as he lived because it was the first time he'd ever used a blooper pitch in a game.

It seemed like months ago, but it had only been a week! He sure hoped Kirk didn't use him tomorrow. He was too stiff! Every muscle in his body ached. He probably wouldn't even be able to find the plate.

CLUTCH HITTER

His mind wandered back to last night. He guessed nothing could be much worse than that! Bobby had maneuvered him around to the Steelers' Recreation Center and the dance. That had been something! The first time in his life he had ever tried to dance—and with Peggy Armstrong at that!

Peggy Armstrong's wide brown eyes had been compelling, no question about that, and in spite of all of Chip Hilton's protests, she and Bobby had persuaded him to dance. He guessed stumbled was a better description of it!

It hadn't been too bad, except for Duck Tucker. Tucker was a good dancer and hadn't even bothered to hide what a kick he was getting out of watching Chip's clumsy movements as he tried to move in time with the music. But Peggy Armstrong hadn't seemed to mind. Peggy, Bobby, and Chip had sat out several dances, and Chip had enjoyed that a lot. His biggest moment of the evening had come when the three of them were talking and Tucker had swaggered over and asked Peggy for a dance.

Peggy had gently placed her hand on Chip's before she had answered Tucker. "No, thanks, Duck. We've got a lot of baseball we want to talk about."

Tucker's glare had brought a chuckle from Bobby, who couldn't resist a jab. "Remember to touch all the bases, Duck," he'd said.

The memory of that evening was a lot more pleasant than the anticipation of the evening in front of him, but at least Tuesday would make up for everything. Peggy had made a date to meet Bobby and Chip for lunch in the cafeteria.

Chip let out a weary sigh and started for the field. As he opened the gate at the grandstand, Kirk's bellow greeted him.

"PRETTY BOY"

"All right, Hilton. Let's go! Get out there on the hill and throw 'em in. Get a move on! Maybe we should have H. L. Armstrong pick you up after work so you could get out here for practice on time!"

Chip got out on the mound and hurled them in although every pitch brought a groan to his lips. His arm and back muscles were so tight he could scarcely lob the ball across the plate, much less put anything on it. After half an hour of batting practice, Kirk called for fielding and then sent Chip to the showers.

"You'll be starting tomorrow afternoon, Hilton," he bellowed, "and I don't want no alibis. Just strikes!"

After practice, Chip went straight home to his rented room at Mrs. Pecora's. He felt completely homesick, discouraged, and unappreciated. For the first time since he had arrived in Mansfield, he was on the verge of packing up and striking out for Valley Falls and the comforts of home.

Mrs. Pecora sensed Chip's depressed mood and gave him the space she knew he needed. This friendly little Italian woman had already become important to Chip. She had raised two sons of her own and now had a couple of grandsons, as well. Mr. Pecora had died a few years after retiring from the steel mill. Now, next to visits from her children and grandchildren, Mrs. Pecora found her greatest pleasure in any happiness she could bring to the people who rented the five available rooms upstairs in her large, old house.

She was a good listener for Chip and a wonderful cook. Chip couldn't resist her homemade ravioli. Their dinner conversation had made a difference, and before he went upstairs to his room for the night, he was feeling more like himself again. Some of his usual positive outlook had returned.

CLUTCH HITTER

Bobby picked him up early in the morning, and they checked in for work together. Chip's new friend was bubbling over with game enthusiasm and payday exuberance. Every time he saw Chip that morning, he cautioned him, "Take it easy! Take it easy! You gotta be right this afternoon."

Mansfield's Steeler Field was located three blocks from H. L. Armstrong's main plant. The field had once belonged to the city, but when Mansfield had constructed its new City Stadium, Armstrong had bought the field with its grandstand as a part of his community recreational program. The city government was delighted to have this older facility used by community groups and maintained by Armstrong's company.

It was a real baseball day, not too hot, yet warm enough to work up a good sweat easily; perspiration does something to sore muscles and aching bones. The crowd, however, was small. The spectators were mostly men from the Yard who had come out to see the new, young pitcher. Five defeats in a row had discouraged all but the most rabid Steelers fans. But, as for every game, the first box to the right of the Steelers dugout was occupied by H. L. and Peggy Armstrong.

Between warm-up throws, Chip inspected the sparse crowd. That is, until he caught sight of Peggy Armstrong. Then, for the first time, he felt conspicuous. Barber was taking Chip's throws when Peggy and her father entered their box. The irrepressible substitute waved his big glove at the dark-haired girl in the yellow linen dress.

Chip wished he could feel as free and confident as Bobby did where girls were concerned. But girls had never meant all that much in his young life, except maybe as chemistry lab partners, athletes, cheerleaders, members of the band, or as reporters for the *Yellow*

Jacket. He also had felt out of place around girls. He laughed. Soapy had said that girls were usually in the way and that a lot of them talked too much. Of course, anything that came between Soapy and food or a game was in the way.

Three o'clock came too soon, much too soon. Chip wasn't ready. He didn't feel right. But Kirk was adamant and the umpire announced the batteries: "For the Fitzgerald Painters: Burns and Hickman! For the Mansfield Steelers: Hilton and Dillon. Play ball!"

The Steelers trotted onto the field, and Chip walked slowly to the mound. But there was no pep, no feeling of delight or urge to play. This was no good. That dull ache of loneliness and discouragement swept through him again.

Only a single voice sounding across the diamond signaled team spirit. Bobby Barber was chattering with all his might. "Let's go, guys! Come on, Chip! Mow 'em down! Mow 'em down!"

But Chip Hilton wasn't able to do any mowing that day. He couldn't find the plate. That little bit of extra smoothness was gone from his delivery and with it the timing that meant control. His arm and shoulder were full of kinks. To make it worse, Dillon's return throws were rifled back to Chip with burning speed. They came speeding back, low, high, to the side, and everywhere but the place for an easy catch.

Chip walked the first two men, and managed to strike out the third batter, but after getting behind to the cleanup hitter, he split the plate with one, letter high, and Fitzgerald had three runs.

And it seemed as though the Painters scored three runs every inning. Chip, who had tried his best to figure out the individual weaknesses of the Painters' hitters when they came to bat, was often surprised at the pitches Dillon called for. But he never shook the surly catcher off. He pitched according to the signs.

(Later, when he was on the bus on the way home to Valley Falls, Chip started to wonder about some of those signs. Could it be possible? But even then he couldn't bring himself to believe that Dillon would have him pitch to a hitter's strength. No, that made no sense!)

The Painters' hurler, Burns, was as good as Chip was bad, and inning by inning the Steelers came apart at the seams. The fielding went bad, and plays that should have been easy outs became costly errors. But Chip never quit. He stayed in there doing the best he could, taking it on the chin as he'd never had to before.

Once, when Buster Dillon had called time and stalked to the dugout, raging at Kirk and demanding that Chip be sent to the showers, Chip dug a small hole in the yellow clay behind the mound with the metal toe of his right shoe. Then he carefully filled it up again. A slight grin flickered across his thin lips as he pictured the Brownings' dog, Shep, smoothing the ground with his nose over the resting place of a bone in the backyard Hilton Athletic Club. But the smile disappeared and with it the fleeting thoughts of Valley Falls and home as Buster Dillon's sneering voice rang out above the crowd.

"All right, pretty boy, let's go!"

The Yard supporters picked up on "pretty boy" then and let Chip have it full blast. Many of them had been hopeful when they had heard about the new, young pitcher, but that hope completely dissolved with the mounting score. They were thoroughly disheartened now, anxious to pin their bitterness and frustration on someone. So they followed Buster Dillon's lead and showered Chip with scornful ridicule.

"Back to Valley Falls, pretty boy!"

"Back to grade school for you!"

"Take him out! Put in the ball boy!"

"Send him to the showers. Put his head in a barrel!"

"Take him out, Kirk, take him out!"

But Gunner Kirk wasn't going to take Chip Hilton out of *that* game. The kid had been too fresh, just too full of himself, and the grouchy manager meant to teach the squirt a good lesson. He figured a poor showing by the kid might also give him an edge with H. L. Armstrong the next time he asked for a pitcher in their on-going baseball discussions.

Chip stopped looking at the scoreboard after the top of the sixth. The Painters were out in front 16-3 then and still going strong. But everything has an ending, and Chip was on his feet and on his way to the locker room under the grandstand almost before Joe Ferris had swung from his heels for the third strike in the bottom of the ninth. Chip Hilton was going home! Tonight was the night! He was outta here!

CHAPTER 7

Whistling in the Dark

MARY HILTON'S son was home and she felt great! Chip's mom greeted him with tears misting her happy, gray eyes. She had missed Chip keenly. There were just the two of them now since Chip's dad had been killed in a pottery accident several years ago, and before this summer, Chip and his mom had been separated only two or three days at a time. She knew Chip's summer away from home was giving her a taste of what was ahead for her a year down the road when Chip would head off to college.

Chip's letters from Mansfield had been so cheerful and confident she'd worried that maybe he didn't need her anymore. She'd been surprised at the strange ache in her heart. Surprised and a little ashamed too. After all, she wanted Chip to be independent; she realized she just wasn't quite ready for it.

Now, one quick glance into Chip's unhappy eyes was enough to reassure her. He'd only been "whistling in the dark," the way he'd done when he was a little boy and scared and needed to act braver than he really felt. Mary Hilton read something, sensed something, even deeper than homesickness in her son's tender eyes. Something else was going on that was troubling Chip. *Well, he'll tell me when he's settled in. It's great to have him home!*

When Chip had first gotten home, he'd picked his mom up and swung her around, her shoulder-length blond hair bouncing with the movement, until she'd laughed her deep, rich laugh and made him put her down. Blushing as she always did, she patted her hair, pretended to frown, and asked her son if he wanted to hear what was happening with all his friends.

She started with the Sugar Bowl where Chip had worked so long. John Schroeder, the owner and the friend who had been so kind to Chip all through the years following Big Chip's death, came first—then Biggie Cohen, Speed Morris, Soapy Smith, who had taken over Chip's job for the summer, and last but not least, Petey Jackson, the soda fountain manager and sports guru.

Mary Hilton's daily travel to her office as a supervisor at the phone company made it easy for her to keep in touch with them, and Doc Jones had stopped by her office to ask about Chip nearly every afternoon. (She had laughed and remarked that Doc needed a few more patients to keep him busy.) All Chip's friends had dropped by the house from time to time, and Taps and Suzy Browning, from next door, had been over every night. One night they'd even brought Shep, who had to fight off Hoops, the Hilton cat who didn't take too kindly to canine visitors.

"Taps misses you so much, Chip," she said softly. "Hoops keeps him company when he drops over to shoot baskets almost every evening."

So, the two of them, along with an insistent Hoops, spent a happy evening together sharing dinner and catching up on all the news in that quiet, small-family companionship they'd always shared and which Chip now greatly needed. As they talked and laughed together, Chip's feelings of depression and frustration evaporated. At last, Chip climbed the stairs, undressed, and drifted off to sleep, content in his own bed. The harshness and soreness in his mind and body passed from him under the encouragement of his mother's love and the peacefulness of familiar surroundings.

It was great coming downstairs to have breakfast with his mom and enjoying the comfort of home. Money wasn't everything. Right after church, he'd tell her about his new plans. The trip home had given him time to think. He'd get a job with the State Highway Department. Why should he be pushed around by men like Kirk and Dillon and Tucker? He didn't need a job *that* bad.

But Chip didn't have a chance to tell his mother anything. Someone had heard he was home, and word spread rapidly. The crew wasn't going to miss seeing a special friend. Biggie Cohen, Speed Morris, Soapy Smith, Taps Browning, and even little Paddy Jackson dropped by to tell him what was up and to find out how he was getting along. They already knew about the game. They had read the brief box score in the *News* and the *Times,* but they avoided mentioning it. Chip brought it up himself. He didn't say anything about his work-stiffened muscles and the job, but he avoided none of the painful details about baseball.

"Guess I'm slipping," he said simply.

"They don't need pitching," Soapy Smith growled. "They need some fielding and hitting!"

"See where you've got a doubleheader tomorrow afternoon," Speed said, trying to change the subject.

WHISTLING IN THE DARK

"Yes," Chip nodded. "The Steelers are playing Ritter Automotive on their field. Plant's closed on account of the Fourth—"

"You pitching?" Soapy asked.

"No," Chip said shortly. "No, I'm not pitching."

Later, Soapy jumped to his feet to help Mary Hilton bring out a double chocolate cake, which the boys pretty much demolished in record speed. Then Soapy said he had to leave but returned in a few minutes with a big package.

"Chip," he stammered, "we, well, all of us got together and bought you this warm-up jacket so you wouldn't forget us whenever the goin' gets a little tough."

That night, a tall, grim-faced teenager sat on the bus back to Mansfield holding a red-and-white warm-up jacket in his lap. The long fingers of his right hand gently traced the words sewn on the inside: *To Chip. From Biggie, Soapy, Speed, Taps, and Petey.*

The next afternoon, Gunner Kirk got the shock of his life. His mouth dropped open and he gazed at Chip in amazement. "You *can't* pitch today!" he echoed. "Why? *Now* what's the matter?"

"I just can't pitch today, Mr. Kirk, that's all," Chip replied quietly.

"But you've *got* to pitch today!" Kirk barked angrily. "We're playin' a double-header. This is a holiday, the Fourth of July, and everybody in the plant and almost everybody in town is here. Are you crazy?"

"No, I'm not crazy, Mr. Kirk, but I pitched Saturday and it's too soon—"

Kirk moved close to Chip's side, his dark face flushed with anger. "You call that pitchin'? That exhibition you dared to make us suffer through? Look at this crowd.

CLUTCH HITTER

Everyone from the mill's over here at Ritter Field. We got a good chance to knock 'em off twice and get back in the runnin'. You scared, kid?"

"No," Chip replied quietly, "I'm not scared, Mr. Kirk. I just don't want to hurt my arm."

Buster Dillon had sensed something was up and approached just in time to hear Chip's last remark. "What arm?" he sneered. "Are you kiddin'? You're gettin' to be a real joke, kid!"

Chip disregarded Dillon completely. "I'm sorry, Mr. Kirk," he said, "but I promised my coach I wouldn't pitch without three days' rest. I'll be all right by Wednesday."

"You'll be all right by Wednesday! Well isn't that just dandy! And what am I supposed to do today? Call off one of the games just because you're not in the mood to pitch? Nothin' doing! You're goin' on the mound today!"

But Chip steadfastly held his ground and refused to pitch. "I'll pitch Wednesday, Mr. Kirk, but I'm not pitching today for you or anyone else. That's final!"

"I'll say it's final," Kirk snarled, turning toward Dillon and Tucker standing a short distance away. "Hilton, I'll take care of you tomorrow. Get down in that dugout and stay out of my sight! You're nothing but a quitter!"

"What's happenin'?" Dillon asked.

Kirk's voice was choked with rage. "Hilton says he won't pitch unless he has three days' rest—"

Dillon whirled toward the dugout. "Why that little squirt!" he raged. "Someone ought to—" He turned on Kirk incredulously. "You gonna take that from that kid? You gonna let him get away with that—"

"What can I do?" Kirk interrupted. "The Old Man hired him. I never saw the kid before last Tuesday. I gotta be careful until I know what the connection is."

WHISTLING IN THE DARK

"So that's it," Tucker mused half-aloud. "That's why the kid is so sure of himself. Now I begin to see the light!"

"What light?" Dillon growled. "What you talkin' about?"

Tucker shook his head. "Nothing. Just something that happened in the cafeteria last week."

"Forget about last week," Dillon muttered. "What're we gonna do this afternoon?"

"Well, *I'm* not going to work," Tucker said coldly, eyeing Kirk. "You told me yesterday you'd let me rest until Wednesday. You said you wanted to save me to pitch against the Mackins."

Duck's cool announcement completely upset Kirk. He turned the full force of his anger upon Tucker. "Listen, Tucker," he said heatedly, "we've got to play two games this afternoon. You and Softy are the only pitchers I've got besides the squirt. You're gonna pitch this afternoon!"

"Then call one of the games off!"

"Are you nuts? We'll call nothin' off. You pitch the second game. Buster, warm up Simmons—"

But Tucker wasn't giving up. "How about yesterday?" he persisted. "Fourteen innings and Buster made me bear down all the way. Just for a measly hundred bucks. Besides, my arm's tired. I'm not feeling right."

It was Dillon's turn to get into the argument now. "Duck, cut that stuff," he growled. "You wanted that extra money as much as anyone else."

Kirk stepped between the angry battery mates. "Not so loud," he muttered. "Do you two want everyone in the park to hear you?" He gripped Tucker's arm and cajoled, "Come on, Duck. Work this one and try to get by Wednesday. I know it's tough, but we all need the money. Look, if you can get by Wednesday, it'll give me a chance to work you regularly for the Wednesday games and that'll leave you free to cash in on all the Sunday games and the easy money. Get it?"

Gunner Kirk may not have been the most astute baseball manager in the world, but he knew Duck Tucker like a book. Tucker was the kind of athlete Kirk labeled as having all style and no substance. He worried about his image and liked trendy clothes and a pocketful of money. Physically, Tucker was built strong and his body was muscular, but if you studied his face closely, the lack of character reflected in the weak chin, the sharp, brown eyes, and the greedy mouth was not flattering.

Duck Tucker had been spoiled by too much sports adulation, too much athletic success, and too much pampering. The overindulgence had all gone to his head. The promise of future Sunday earnings did the trick. Tucker sullenly agreed to work the second game.

Kirk smiled grimly. Someday he'd have his own innings with this college prima donna, and he promised himself the satisfaction of making this professional amateur get down on his knees and beg for money.

Simmons was no pitcher, and the Steelers fans knew it. When the umpire announced the battery and Softy walked out to the mound, a wave of protest swept through the stands.

"No! No!"

"Not Simmons again! We'll even take Hilton over him."

"We want our money back!"

But Simmons worked, and the Ritter batters fattened their batting averages at the expense of sorrowful pitching that didn't rate even by Little League standards. The Steelers didn't quit, but the odds were too great. They could never catch up with the score. Simmons tried hard, but he just didn't have what it takes to be a successful hurler. The game was a debacle. Ritter whacked Simmons all over the park. The final score was 17-12.

The second game wasn't much better. The Steelers stands took heart when Tucker was announced as the starting pitcher, but Duck was too tired and overused. The fourteen-inning stint the day before had taken too much out of his arm, and the lowly Ritters swept through the second game of the double header much as they had the first, winning 9-4.

Tucker hadn't pulled his pitches. He was trying to impress the Armstrongs, and so he gave all he had, but it just wasn't enough. He couldn't find the corners, and when he tried to call on his fastball in the clutches, it just wasn't there. He had played himself out.

As the crowd filed out of Ritter Field, Steelers supporters took a terrific razzing from the happy Ritter crowd. It looked as though the Ritters might go places after all! Weren't the Steelers supposed to be the class of the league? Next to the Mackins?

"Soft steel!"

"What happened?"

"Where'd ya get that lame bunch of clowns?"

"Better get the *whole* State team!"

The Steelers fans ignored the Ritter supporters completely. They had their own particular targets—the entire Steelers ball club. And they got on every Steeler in sight. Gunner Kirk caught most of the abuse. He wasn't popular to begin with, and the real fans had begun to second-guess his masterminding.

Kirk was boiling inside, but he controlled himself. Then he remembered Armstrong. The boss always stayed behind to have a brief chat with Kirk after every game, at home or away. And he was there today, waiting with his daughter at the grandstand.

CLUTCH HITTER

Armstrong knew baseball, and he knew something was drastically wrong with this team. He wasted no time in voicing the question uppermost in his mind.

"Why didn't you use the Hilton boy, Kirk?"

Kirk stiffened, glanced at Peggy Armstrong, and then answered hesitantly. "Why—er—that's what I wanted to talk to you about, Mr. Armstrong. You see, er— Well, Hilton needs a little disciplining. He's missed several practices, and he's been actin' a bit high and mighty. Most of the other players are beginning to resent him."

Kirk eyed Armstrong trying to see how his words were affecting the big boss. But Armstrong's searching brown eyes revealed nothing. A somewhat worried Kirk was forced to continue.

"I asked him to pitch today, sir, but—um—he said he had promised his coach not to pitch more than once every three days."

Armstrong nodded. "Oh, I see. Well, he has something *there,* hasn't he, Kirk?"

"Yes, he's a strong kid, but when I was playin' ball we worked every day!"

"Playing and pitching are a little different. By the way, couldn't you plan your pitching assignments a little better? The games are fairly well-spaced, and you should be able to get along with three pitchers."

"Yes, sir, but we don't have three pitchers. We don't even have two."

"Then you're not sure Hilton can help us. Is that it?"

Kirk played his part well. "No, sir, you know how it is with a kid who gets too much publicity. It goes to his head. Maybe ridin' the bench will straighten him out."

H. L. Armstrong's face showed his disappointment at Kirk's words. "Temperamental, eh? I'm surprised. He seemed like such a nice young man. It's a pity, but I guess some kids have to go through that stage. I sure hope you can straighten the youngster out. He's the protégé of one of my best friends, and I want you to give him a lot of attention."

Kirk nodded, feigning concern. "I'll do the best I can."

Armstrong cast an embarrassed glance at the scoreboard and shook his head. "By the way, Tucker didn't look too good today. He really looked tired. I've been wondering why you didn't use him Saturday. Then you could have had him ready for the Mackins this Wednesday."

Armstrong paused, his keen eyes watching Kirk intently. Kirk reddened. He was caught, and for a few seconds he couldn't come up with an answer. Then he took the only possible out.

"His arm's sore, Mr. Armstrong. It's been botherin' him for a couple of weeks. He's been pitchin' his heart out, Mr. Armstrong, for batting practices and then the games too. He's overworked."

Armstrong pulled a little schedule card out of his pocket and studied it carefully. "Let's see," he pondered half-aloud, "Tucker hasn't pitched since June 22nd. That was against the Mackins. And this is the Fourth of July. That's twelve days' rest, Kirk. That doesn't seem much like overwork to me! Send Tucker around to Doctor Carter in the morning."

Peggy Armstrong was unusually quiet on the ride home. Her father attributed her silence to the double defeat and was busy with his own thoughts. Peggy was thinking about Chip Hilton and Duck Tucker, thinking that maybe she had misjudged them both. Chip Hilton hadn't seemed temperamental or arrogant, and she certainly had never thought of Duck Tucker as self-sacrificing. It was certainly easy to misjudge people. Maybe she ought to be a little nicer to Duck.

CHAPTER 8

Come up Smiling

GUNNER KIRK closed the door to the small room that he used as the baseball office in the recreation building and turned to Duck Tucker.

"Look, Duck," he said earnestly, "if you play this up good and string the doctor along, we'll be OK. Ain't no one, not even the doctor, can tell you about how your arm feels, except you."

Tucker was rebellious. "Gunner," he said defiantly, "there's nothing wrong with my arm. Nothing a little rest won't cure. I shouldn't have pitched two days in a row, and I'm not going to do it again for you or anyone else!"

"Well, who's gonna do it if you don't? Softy Simmons has quit—not that he ever was any good anyways—and the squirt hasn't shown us a thing. Remember, you ain't been winnin' for the Steelers, even if you have been goin' good at Glendale. Remember, too, Armstrong gave you a job here for the past two summers because you're a pitcher. That means you gotta do a little pitchin' for the

Steelers. Now we can both have an alibi for the team lookin' so bad if you can pull the wool over Doc Carter's eyes. You been pitchin' your arm off and your heart out, see? All for the Steelers! And Doc Carter will tell that to the Old Man, and he'll think you're a hero."

Kirk watched Tucker intently. He could see Duck was half-sold, so he used his clincher. "Besides, Duck, I told Armstrong you was burned up because we'd been losin' and you was workin' too hard in the practices, get it? Another thing, Peggy Armstrong believes everything her old man says about sports and he'll tell her for certain. You wouldn't mind havin' her thinkin' you was a hero now, would you?"

Duck Tucker was proud of his pitching ability. His arm was fine—just tired. He knew his baseball future depended on taking care of his arm. Now he was angry with himself. He'd been risking his arm and a future major-league career for mere pennies. Pennies! He bitterly bawled himself out for his stupidity. From now on, he'd pitch twice a week, he resolved, and no more! One game for the Steelers, and one for Kirk to get his Sunday payoff.

"All right," he muttered, "all right, I'll go see Carter." On the way to the plant dispensary, Tucker continued to kick himself for his foolishness in getting mixed up with a man like Kirk. "Buster Dillon, too," he muttered. "And I must have been crazy to let Coach Bennett talk me into coming down here to this measly jerk job just so I could keep pitching all summer. What did I have to gain? I could have pitched Sunday ball and made my money just the same and partied the rest of the week."

Del Bennett was the state university's baseball coach. He had been a major-league pitching star and he knew baseball inside and out. But more importantly, he knew his athletes. He recognized Duck Tucker for just what he was—an athlete who was endowed with lots of physical abilities but little or no sense of responsibility. Bennett had hoped an off-season opportunity in which his star hurler could pitch amateur ball and hold down a summer job at the same time might awaken in the spoiled young athlete a realization of the values in life that were just as important—no, more important!—than baseball. The report of the first summer hadn't been too good from the work side, but it had kept Tucker out of trouble and kept him doing the thing he liked best, pitching baseball.

Tucker's steps slowed as he approached Carter's office, but he forced himself to keep the appointment. Carter examined Tucker's arm quickly and efficiently, but he was puzzled. The arm wasn't inflamed, there was no throbbing, and his deft fingers searched with futility for any unusual swelling.

"I don't think there's anything much wrong with your arm, Tucker," he said thoughtfully. "Probably a good rubdown and a few days of heat lamp and rest will fix it up as good as ever."

Carter studied Tucker's evasive brown eyes for an instant. "I'm sure the arm's all right, aren't you?"

Tucker shook his head. "No. I'm certain there's something wrong with it, Doc. It's just not right."

A brief smile crossed Carter's lips. Then he continued softly, "There's nothing for you to worry about, Tucker. That arm's OK."

Tucker may not have had anything to worry about, but Chip Hilton had plenty to disturb him. Kirk, Tucker, and Dillon had spread the word that the high school squirt had refused to pitch the day before and that he was responsible for the twin loss to the Ritters, the weakest team in the league.

COME UP SMILING

Barber had walked to work with Chip that morning, and the two friends matched strides in near silence.

"The going will be tough today, Chip," Bobby said anxiously.

"I know, Bobby."

And tough it was. Although Jake Miller was understanding, the Yard work crew seemed to have lost all respect for the new pitcher. There were no smiles, and only a few of the older men even took the trouble to greet him. Chip worked in silence, with a gathering resentment in his heart. How much could a guy take?

Bobby met Chip as the noon siren finished its wail. "Come on," he said with forced enthusiasm, "let's go to the cafeteria for lunch. I've got a taste for some ice cream!"

Chip smiled. "Oh, sure," he said knowingly. "I'll take vanilla!"

"I thought you would," Barber said, lifting an eyebrow. "With or without?"

"Without what?"

"You know what!"

Chip grinned. He guessed he knew, all right. He guessed he knew, too, that Bobby Barber was just as anxious to keep the lunch date with Peggy Armstrong as he was.

Well, Peggy Armstrong was there, all right. So was Duck Tucker. They were sitting together at a table and just starting on their dessert—vanilla ice cream smothered in hot chocolate fudge.

"Hey, check that out!" Bobby turned surprised eyes on Chip. "She must have forgot."

They passed right by the table, and Bobby flashed Peggy his warmest smile. "Hi ya, Peggy," he said, ignoring Tucker. "Did you forget about us?"

"Oh, yes, Bobby," Peggy said, "I'm afraid I did. I'm awfully sorry though."

She turned back to Tucker, barely nodding to Chip, her cold attitude clearly indicating she had nothing more to say to them about anything. But Tucker couldn't resist this opportunity. He could scarcely restrain himself.

"Well, I forgot about you, too, Bobby," he said loudly. "As a matter of fact, I forgot about both of you, or at least I'm trying to! Remember, don't knock over any trays or tables now, you guys. You don't want to get those nice blue overalls dirty!"

Bobby's mouth hung half-open and he turned to Chip with a demoralized grin. "Well, what d'ya know about that!" he managed.

"Let's get out of here! I'm not hungry anymore," Chip said shortly.

Barber glowered at Tucker darkly. "Now won't be soon enough for me," he said with repressed anger. He stood there a moment or so looking straight into Tucker's eyes. "Someday, Tucker," he said deliberately, "I'm gonna wipe that conceited, arrogant smile off your face. Job or no job!"

Chip Hilton scarcely heard Tucker's insulting remark or his friend's angry rejoinder. He found himself staring into Peggy Armstrong's lovely brown eyes. He didn't realize he was staring until he saw her blush and turn her eyes away. There was a great deal that Chip Hilton did not know about girls.

His job at the Sugar Bowl during the three years he had spent so far in high school took up most of his evenings, and what little time was left went into his books and athletics. Maybe he should take Soapy's view; he always regarded girls as just a lot of noise and nuisance. Now he knew Soapy had been right on that score all along . . . a lot of noise and nuisance! All of them! Just the same, the special day he had looked forward to had suddenly turned out to be a total bust.

But the worst was yet to come. At four o'clock, Chip hurried to meet Bobby at the Yard tool house. But Bobby wasn't alone. Big Nose and thirty or forty other men were waiting too. It was unusual for men coming off a shift to hang around before going home. Chip had noticed the men, but he didn't think much of it until he was even with the group and Big Nose greeted him.

"You in a hurry, Hilton?"

"Why, no, Pig Iron. I'm just going over to practice."

"Then can you spare us a couple of minutes?"

"Why, sure . . . sure!"

"We thought you could," someone said dryly.

"Yeah," Big Nose continued, "we're gonna hold Yard Court and we want you to take part. The leading part! You're on trial!"

"Yard Court!"

"Hey, Yard Court!"

Shouts rang out from all sides, and Chip was surrounded and rushed to the loading platform. He went along without resistance, weakly trying to smile. "What's the charge?" he asked.

"Loafin' on the job," someone growled. "Loafin' on the job and on the ballfield."

Chip's trial was short. Big Nose asked who was for the defendant, and Bobby Barber pushed through the crowd and leaped to the platform.

"What's the charge?"

There were plenty of accusers. It seemed to Chip that everyone had something to say.

"Refusin' to play ball!"

"Layin' down on the team!"

"Being a big shot and too good to pitch!"

Big Nose quieted the barrage of shouts. "What's the defense?" he asked Bobby.

"It's a false charge," Bobby shouted. "There's no truth to it—"

But Bobby was drowned out by cries of "Guilty!" Big Nose raised his arms. "For the prosecution?" he shouted.

There wasn't any doubt about the feelings of the crowd. Chip Hilton was guilty! The roar was deafening.

"For the defense?"

Again that unbelievable quiet followed, and angry as he was, Chip marveled at the deep silence. Big Nose's shout "Guilty!" charged the crowd into action, and Chip was dragged off the platform and doused roughly in the trough. Not once, but twenty times. He wasn't alone. Barber was dunked too. Just for good measure.

Chip came up smiling each time, but it wasn't a pretty smile. There was no humor in the wide-set gray eyes. Later, as Chip and Bobby, soaked to the skin and feeling down, walked silently to Steeler Field, both were filled with bitter thoughts.

Chip was prepared for anything when he followed Bobby through the gate at the grandstand. In fact, he was hoping for a way to end this summer nightmare and to tell Kirk, Dillon, or Tucker where to get off.

But Gunner Kirk surprised him. The slick manager hadn't forgotten H. L. Armstrong's instructions and greeted Chip with a sugary half-smile. "How about throwin' 'em in for the hitters, kid," he said impersonally.

Kirk had made up his mind to go along with the new pitcher until he could get the connection between Armstrong and Hilton, until he could find out for sure just why Armstrong was interested in the kid. But that hadn't kept Kirk from backstabbing Chip by instructing

Dillon and Tucker to pour it on the fresh high school kid.

Dillon was an expert "jockey." He enjoyed riding a guy, and Chip Hilton got the full benefit of Buster's years of experience. Dillon caught the batting practice and burned the return throws back to Chip with every ounce of his power. Several times Chip simply stepped aside and let the speeding ball fly past him to the outfield. Tucker followed Dillon's lead and made sly remarks about a certain high school pitcher who seemed better suited for a Boy Scout uniform than a baseball uniform.

Between hitting turns, Duck Tucker sat alone glowering in the dugout. He watched the free, easy delivery Chip used so well, and deep animosity for the high school star, which had been growing in Tucker's heart, burned more deeply than ever—especially after the lunch incident when he had seen Peggy Armstrong blush at Chip's stare. Then he saw Chip's red-and-white warm-up jacket folded neatly at the end of the bench. He surreptitiously lit a cigarette and moved down near the jacket. Chip saw Tucker sitting there in the dugout, but it meant nothing at the time. After a few minutes, Tucker trotted out to the field to catch some flies with the outfielders.

Later, Kirk called for infield practice, and Chip hurried over to get his warm-ups before joining the outfielders. He dropped down into the dugout and reached for the jacket. Then he saw the holes. Holes that had burned clear through the front of the jacket. Ugly cigarette holes. Seven of them! Seven holes that someone had deliberately burned through the cloth.

Chip stood there holding the jacket in his hands, and suddenly it came to him that he had taken as much as he could take. He had turned the other cheek as much as he could. He was not going to allow himself to be pushed around anymore by Tucker, Dillon, and Kirk. He had reached his limit.

He didn't put on the jacket, just dropped his glove, and, trailing the jacket on the ground, marched straight out to right field where Tucker was chasing flies.

"Did you burn the holes in this warm-up jacket?"

A brief, sadistic smile flashed across one side of Tucker's mouth as he studied Chip's set face. "And what if I did, squirt? What are you gonna do about it? Tell your coach?" he sneered.

Chip drove a hard right so suddenly to Tucker's jaw that the surprise of the blow left the star pitcher's mouth half-open in amazement. Chip followed with a left to the stomach. Tucker grunted and dropped his hands, and Chip flailed both hands to the head. Tucker backtracked with Chip right after him. Up against the fence, Tucker grappled with Chip, and the two wrestled to the ground.

The encounter amazed everyone, but as the two fighting figures fell to the ground, other players dashed up and pulled them apart.

"What's the matter with you two guys?"

"Break it up!"

"Knock it off!"

Tucker struggled to get at Chip, his face contorted with rage. "Let me go! Let me at him!" he thundered as he was gripped by the shoulders.

"That's not a real bright idea, Duck," chuckled one of the Steelers holding him. "It looks like you're a better pitcher than you are a fighter."

Chip waited silently, his gray eyes narrowed into small slits and his thin lips compressed in a straight line. But he made no struggle to free himself from the restraining hands of the other players. He'd do his fighting with his hands and not with his mouth.

COME UP SMILING

Kirk came puffing up, followed closely by Dillon. "If you guys want to fight, you fight off the field! There'll be no fighting here!" Kirk commanded.

"That suits me just fine," Chip said quietly. "Anytime, Tucker, just anytime and anyplace."

Lefty Curtis put his arm around Chip's shoulder and pulled him away. "C'mon, Hilton," he said persuasively, "forget about it! We don't want to fight among ourselves."

"No," Gunner Kirk snarled, "let's try fightin' to win a game for a change instead of each other!" He added wearily, "That's all for tonight!"

Bobby Barber fell in step with Chip as they walked into the locker room. Neither player spoke. Each was deep in thought.

The hot shower soothed Chip's muscles, but it did little to ease the bitterness in his heart and the anger in his thoughts toward Duck Tucker. The next time there would be a real showdown!

CHAPTER 9

One of the Crew

DAVE MACKIN, president of Mackin Motors, was, as usual, in a convivial mood. His blue eyes were snapping merrily as he proudly identified his favorite ballplayers for H. L. Armstrong.

"Corrigan and Kurt are both warming up," he said proudly. "Looks like we're going to give you both barrels!"

Armstrong forced a wry smile. "One would be enough," he said resignedly. "Tucker has a sore arm."

Mackin nudged Peggy Armstrong and winked. "Your father seems to forget his college star has already pitched against us twice this year and took it on the chin both times."

Mackin, H. L., and Peggy Armstrong were sitting in a box on the third-base side of the infield. H. L. Armstrong was putting on a bold and positive front, smiling cheerfully and talking with enthusiasm. But inside, he was burning up. He'd have given his right arm to make Mackin eat those words. But it was true. Mackin's team had beaten the Steelers twice. Easily!

"Mr. Kirk must be going to pitch Chip," Peggy said and then added hastily, "I mean Hilton, Dad. He's warming up, and Duck is sitting in the dugout."

Mackin's eyes lit up with interest as he studied the athlete loosening up in front of the grandstand. "So that's the young Bill Hilton," he said curiously. "How's he doing, H. L.?"

"Why, not very good, Dave. From what Kirk tells me, he's a little impressed with his own importance and his high school clippings."

Mackin frowned. "No! That's too bad," he said regretfully. "You know, H. L., I knew the boy's father. I was up at State with him! He was a terrific athlete! Played any sport well! You know, the kid's the picture of his father."

Mackin's eyes glazed and his voice softened. "Chip Hilton's kid! Where does the time go?" His face sobered, and his eyes shifted across the diamond where, for several minutes, he concentrated on a well-built teenager dressed in expensive but casual clothes who was standing in front of the Mackin bench. Then he sighed deeply and resumed studying the new Steelers pitcher.

Lefty Kurt started for the Mackins and sat the Steeler hitters down one, two, three. When the Steelers trotted out on the field, there was only a slight burst of applause, and with the exception of Bobby Barber's ringing, "Come on, Chipper," absolutely no encouragement greeted Chip Hilton when he walked slowly to the mound.

But there were plenty of jeers for Chip. Not only from the stands but from the Mackin dugout.

"So *this* is the pretty boy!"

"What happened to your record, Hilton?"

CLUTCH HITTER

"Hey! Hey, Hilton! You forgot your press clippings!"

"Back to high school, pretty boy!"

"Here you go, Hilton! Here you go!"

And go Chip did. He went right through the big end of the Mackin stick. The leadoff hitter tried to get Chip in a hole, tried to work him for a walk. But Chip didn't intend to get behind, and on the two-and-two count, he blazed a sidewinder right across the middle of the plate for a called third strike.

The second hitter topped an easy roller to Shorty Welch on the little second sacker's glove side and was tossed out easily at first. And then the first of the big guns went out on a pop fly to Don Catolono behind third base. And that's the way it went, Kurt handcuffing the Steelers and Chip keeping step.

Chip's crossfire fastball had the Mackin hitters throttled. Repeatedly, he moved the right-handed hitters back from the plate with a high fastball. He followed that with a curve that looked as though it would be a mile inside, but the ball cut away at the last second to catch the outside corner for a called strike. The Mackin first baseman and Lefty Kurt both batted southpaw, but they didn't hit. Chip kept his fastball and his curveball low and inside. That was the ticket.

The Mackins' bats might have been silenced, but their bench jockeys were on Chip's case before and after every pitch.

"Balk! Two steps! Two steps, ump!"

"Double windup!"

"Steppin' away from the batter!"

"Hitch in the stretch! You blind, ump?"

The chief baiter in the Mackin dugout wasn't even in uniform. Chip glanced at him once, noting only that the mouthy fan was about his own age and dressed in flashy sports clothes. But Chip was scarcely aware of the words the kid shouted, barely conscious of the bench jockeying. He was feeling right today and he knew it! And he was fired by a burning drive concerned with one, and only one, urgent desire—to win this game!

Behind the plate, Dillon squatted, gave the sign, thumped his glove, and chattered away. At first, his booming "Pretty boy!" brought laughter and numerous echoes from the Mackin and the Steelers fans alike. But as inning after inning passed and Chip steadily mowed the opposing hitters down, Buster Dillon's sarcasm changed to "Atta boy, kid," and "Come on, baby! You can strike 'em out!"

At first, it was a cautious, reluctant change, but gradually, in spite of himself, in spite of his dislike for the high school squirt, the burly receiver warmed to Chip's masterly performance.

And all at once, something clicked with the Steelers ball club. The chatter picked up and took on a more confident air, the ball-handling came sure and sharp, and when they came to bat, the hitters were a little tougher to put away. Kurt had held the Steelers to three scattered hits, and Chip had allowed only two singles going into the top of the ninth.

Dillon hadn't come within a mile of hitting the ball all day. Kurt had Buster's number. So when the swaggering catcher led off, Dillon changed his tactics at the plate. Instead of trying to kill the ball, he crowded the plate, backed out of the box, stepped back in, played cat-and-mouse with Kurt until the left-hander began to burn. All the time, Dillon kept up a steady flow of taunting remarks.

"Come on, Dirty-Girty-Kurty, push one in here!"

Kurt pushed one in there, all right. Right into Dillon's ribs. Buster put on a good show then, to the enthusiastic enjoyment of the Steelers stands. He charged toward the mound, shaking his fist and threatening to "kill the bum!" But a bit of persuasion by the umpire convinced Dillon that it wasn't an intentional beanball, and he finally permitted himself to be herded toward first base.

Chip had been on deck. Now he stopped short of the box, knocked a bit of dirt from each shoe, and watched Matt Murphy in the first-base coaching box for the sign. Chip had singled sharply his first time at bat, flied out to deep left center the second trip, and on his third try was out by a step on a hard ground ball that the third baseman gunned to first. But he had been sure he'd get hold of one of Kurt's southpaw slants his next time at bat. Now he felt a little flash of regret. There was only one possible play. Dillon *had* to be moved down to second. He acknowledged Murphy's sign, got Dillon's return sign, and stepped into the box.

Kurt had cooled off by now. He knew the only play possible too. He knew Dillon was a turtle on the base paths, so he kept his pitches high. Too high. Chip looked the first two over, and the count was two balls and no strikes against the Mackin hurler. Then Kurt gunned a low, sharp breaking pitch that cut in toward Chip's ankles. Chip started to draw back, but something clicked in his mind, and instead, he swung viciously. He concentrated on missing the darting ball, feverishly hoping it would get away from the Mackin receiver.

Chip's full cut nearly got a piece of the darting ball and so did the Mackin catcher. But Chip missed it and so did the catcher. The ball spun off the catcher's glove and went skipping clear back against the grandstand. Dillon lumbered down to second base, riding the southpaw with "Dirty-Girty-Kurty" all the way.

ONE OF THE CREW

Chip breathed a sigh of relief and stepped back out of the box. Dillon was safe on second base, and now he could take a full cut and, maybe, win his own game.

But Chip had forgotten about Gunner Kirk. The Steelers manager bellowed, "Time!" Kirk charged out of the dugout and headed for Chip, muttering and scuffing his feet along the ground.

"What's the idea of passin' up the sign? Who do you think you are? Huh? For two cents I'd smack you right in the face! You had to know the sign! You gave it to Dillon yourself! What's the big idea?"

Chip leaned the bat against his leg and deliberately continued his batting ritual. He never said a word, just regarded the irate manager coolly and unflinchingly. That irked Kirk worse than ever. He was so angry that he shook from head to foot. But reason finally got the upper hand. Kirk drew his breath in with a snort, took his cap off his head and banged it across his thigh several times, waved his arms, and strode back to the dugout.

"Play ball!"

Chip glanced at the umpire and again went through his batting ritual. Then he glanced down toward Murphy, still in the first-base coaching box, and got the sign for another bunt.

The sign was right. It was the thing to do. Dillon was slow, and if the Steelers could get the big receiver down to third on a sacrifice, they'd have two chances to get a run across. Especially when the big end of the stick was coming up. But Chip was frustrated. He wanted to hit. Forget about Gunner Kirk and the signs.

He stepped into the box and concentrated on Lefty Kurt. With the count now three and one, the fat pitch had to be coming up.

"Time!"

CLUTCH HITTER

Chip came out of his stance. Now what? But it was the Mackin manager this time. He walked slowly out in front of the mound and went into a huddle with Lefty Kurt. Again Chip stepped out of the box. How long was this going to go on? He knew what that little group in front of the mound was talking about, all right. An intentional pass. The winning run was on second and one more man on base could only help the Mackins. An intentional walk would place men on first and second, and there would be a play at any base, as well as the possibility of a double play.

Chip didn't look at Matt Murphy this time before stepping back into the box. He was on his own. Not because of any of Gunner Kirk's strategy but because Chip Hilton was going to win his own game if he could—if that ball came anywhere near the plate!—even if he had to fight Gunner Kirk, Buster Dillon, Duck Tucker, and the whole Steelers outfit.

The Mackin catcher crouched behind the plate and gave his sign. Kurt took his stretch, lowered the ball to his waist, looked over his left shoulder at the jabbering Steelers catcher dancing about near second base, and then threw wide of the plate. But Kurt was a little too careful not to throw too far away from the plate, and Chip took a chance. He and the Mackin catcher went for the ball almost in unison, but Chip's long bat followed his quick step toward the ball, and he put everything he had into the reaching swing.

The bat met the ball solidly, and Chip took off with every bit of speed at his command. Six steps up the first-base line he lifted his eyes to see the ball heading straight for the right fielder and the right-field fence with the big 325 painted on the wall near the foul line flag.

Chip was in full stride now, stretching his long legs desperately, but it was wasted effort. He could have crawled around the bases so far as that hit was concerned. The ball was over the fence, across the street, on top of somebody's porch. A home run in any ballpark.

Buster Dillon took his time prancing in for the first run of the game, and Chip slackened his speed to go trotting around the base paths accompanied by the first real cheer he had received since he had come to Mansfield.

Don Catolono, in the third-base coaching box, kept shouting, "Touch all the bases, Chip! Touch all the bases!" and then trotted beside Chip all the way to make sure he stomped the plate. Shorty Welch, who had been on deck, Joe Ferris, and Bobby met him there, and one of them snatched off his cap while the Steelers fans stood and cheered him to the skies.

All the way to the dugout, Buster Dillon led the good-natured assault and joined in generally in roughing him up. Only Gunner Kirk and Duck Tucker failed to greet him. The manager kept muttering about "high school squirts who crossed up the signs," and Tucker was harping about "showoff stuff."

"If I pulled that," Tucker griped, "I'd never hear the last of it."

But no one was interested in Duck Tucker. The Steelers were whipping the Mackins, and that was the only thing that counted.

Shorty Welch, the chunky little second baseman, pushed a bunt ahead of him along the first-base line, but the Mackin first baseman swooped in on it and fired the ball to Kurt to beat Shorty by a step. Joe Ferris struck out and Matt Murphy got hold of one, but the Mackin center fielder pulled it in just short of the fence. So the

CLUTCH HITTER

Steelers dashed onto the field for the bottom of the ninth, full of pep and vigor. They owed their two-run lead to a tall, slender high school hurler who had pitched flawless ball for eight innings and had driven in both runs by desperately pushing an intentional pass ball over the fence.

Chip wasn't letting up now. The Mackins never had a chance. He breezed three straight curveballs past the cleanup hitter and used only eight pitches for the two pinch hitters to strike out the last three men to face him.

With the third strike, Steelers fans, who had been holding their breath and pulling for the young pitcher who was winning his own game, let forth with a tremendous cheer. And it was all for the kid. Their kid! Chip scarcely got off the infield before he was mobbed by a cheering, admiring crowd.

Bobby Barber tried to clear the way for Chip, but right in front of the dugout a *Journal* photographer stopped them and asked for a picture. The crowd gave him a lot of good-natured advice, and as they stood there feeling self-conscious and a little silly, Bobby whispered in Chip's ear. "Look who's standing in the box behind of the dugout looking at you!"

Chip glanced that way and saw four people: the Steelers' big boss, as Bobby called H. L. Armstrong, a smiling Peggy Armstrong, a jolly, pleasant fat man, and the loudmouthed sports fan who had been in front of the Mackin dugout throughout the game. The pleasant-faced man was smiling, but the teenager in the bright sports clothes was scowling contemptuously straight at Chip.

"You see that guy with Peggy and the Old Man? The old one?" Bobby asked. "Well, that's Dave Mackin, president of Mackin's. And that's Davy Mackin, his son, standing beside Peggy Armstrong." Barber made a face at Davy

Mackin and then breathed out of the corner of his mouth to Chip. "Davy's a dork! He's the one who was beefin' all through the game about your delivery. A real jerk!"

They pushed through the crowd, down through the dugout, and into the first dressing room the Steelers had used that year that emanated any warmth—a warmth that had nothing to do with walls, floor, lighting, battered lockers, or a heating system. Everyone was talking and laughing, and for the first time, Chip Hilton was accepted as one of the crew.

Gunner Kirk had waited for his usual postgame chat with H. L. Armstrong, and although Buster Dillon and Duck Tucker were in the dressing room, they took no part in the celebration. Tucker was muttering about the lack of support he got whenever he pitched, and Dillon was sitting quietly in front of his locker, gazing blankly at the opposite wall.

Buster Dillon wasn't built for thinking. He was a little too wide between the ears. But one thing was certain about his thinking processes. Once a thought got under way, it had to get out before another even had a chance of entering. Buster Dillon's behavior was entirely out of character, and a few of the happy players glanced his way in surprise. But the big catcher was oblivious to everything but his thoughts about Chip Hilton. He knew now, for sure, something he'd reluctantly feared from the first day he had seen Chip Hilton, from the moment the high school squirt had made him look so bad at the plate. He knew that Chip Hilton had more stuff than any kid he'd ever seen; he was the best big-league prospect he had ever caught. And Dillon's plodding, piece-by-piece mind was busy with a scheme. A scheme that was built around the young hurler's future.

Joe College

BUSTER DILLON, slouched in the back seat of Gunner Kirk's Oldsmobile, was scowling intently at the back of Duck Tucker's head. Occasionally, he glanced through the open car window at the shadowy outlines of flying telephone poles, trees, road intersections, and lighted houses. But always, he returned to his dark study of the back of Tucker's uncovered head.

Behind the wheel, Kirk morosely concentrated on his driving. The Sunday night traffic was heavy, and he was physically and mentally tired. It was 150 miles from Glendale to Mansfield, and Kirk was in a hurry to get home, to get rid of his two companions.

Twenty-four hours in the company of Buster Dillon and Duck Tucker was enough to get the best of any man. He'd be glad when this year was over. It would be Tucker's last season with the Steelers, thank goodness. The temperamental star would graduate from State next spring and undoubtedly sign with some professional team. Maybe Kirk could get rid of Buster too. He'd had a tough time all year with these two troublemakers, keeping them from fighting, trying to keep them happy. It just wasn't worth it.

Tucker was in an angry, nervous mood. First, he slumped against the window, then he sat upright and lit another cigarette. After a few puffs, he snapped it out the window and tried another position. Each time he moved, he sighed in disgust.

"What's the matter, Joe College?" Dillon asked sarcastically. "Got another headache?"

"Only when I look at you," Tucker returned.

Gunner Kirk jammed his foot harder on the accelerator. "Shut up, you two," he growled. "Forget it!"

But Tucker and Dillon weren't the kind to forget the loss of a one-hundred-dollar winning bonus. Not when Glendale was leading 5-3 and had the game wrapped up going into the top of the ninth. Tucker had pitched beautifully until the last frame. Then a walk, a scratch single, and a bunt that Dillon booted had filled the bases. Tucker and Dillon had bellowed at one another about that until Kirk had been forced to call time to cool them off.

The distraught manager finally shut up the two, but the peace didn't last long. With a full count on the next hitter, Tucker shook off three straight signs and Dillon gave up. Then Tucker threw a curve that didn't break soon enough, and the hitter lined a solid triple to deep left center. The hit cleaned the bases, and suddenly, Glendale was one run behind instead of two in front. Glendale didn't get that run back in the bottom of the ninth, and Kirk's star battery didn't get a victory bonus.

It had taken all of Kirk's diplomacy and persuasion to keep Dillon from jumping Tucker after the game. Kirk had pulled Dillon aside and talked to him earnestly.

"Look, Buster," he remonstrated, "we can't afford to have trouble with the guy. He's got us, too, you know. If you hit him and he gets mad and quits, he's just as liable to squeal to Armstrong about us playin' up here as not. He's that kind of a loser, Buster. He'll drag us into any kind of a hole he gets in. Skip it! This is his last year."

Tucker had hoped that Chip's success in the Mackin game had been just one of those things, a fluke. But Chip had shut down Tri-State the following Saturday to win 6-1. Hilton had then relieved Tucker the next Wednesday in the third inning against the Painters with the Steelers behind in the score. He had then gone on to win his own game again in the eighth, with a three-bagger and two aboard. Tucker began to realize he had a serious pitching rival.

Chip had proved he was no flash in the pan by working a great game against Ritter Automotive the following Saturday, going all the way, limiting the opponents to one hit, and leading the Steelers in hitting to win 9-0. That had been Hilton's fourth-straight win.

That game had hurt Tucker most, and he had sulked all afternoon. He almost wished he hadn't agreed to pitch ball every Sunday for Gunner Kirk, Glendale, and money. Now he saw his popularity and importance to the Steelers slipping away almost with every pitch the newcomer made. Near the end of the game, when he saw that nothing short of a miracle could stop Hilton, Tucker had deliberately walked away from the first-base coaching box and headed for the dugout. Buster Dillon had covered up for him and taken his place in the coaching box, but Kirk was hopping mad, and at the end of the inning he stormed into the dugout.

"Take that cigarette out of your mouth," Kirk ordered Tucker. "What's the idea of walkin' away from the coachin' box and makin' me look like some kind of a fool? What's the matter with you? What's gotten into you?"

Tucker made no answer but flipped the stub of the cigarette deliberately on top of Chip's warm-up jacket lying on the bench. It was Kirk who snatched up the windbreaker and shook out the smoldering butt. Then he tore into Tucker full blast.

The Steelers had a ball club now. It was a winning club and a happy club. And the new pitcher was the most popular member of the team. Everything seemed to be going all right for Chip at last. Everything except his friendship with Peggy Armstrong. Chip didn't intend to renew that acquaintance. He would never give any girl a chance to stand him up and embarrass him again! It just seemed to come natural to girls to use the double cross. And the prettier they were, the less a guy could trust them! Soapy was right!

Bobby tried to get Chip to go to the cafeteria for lunch, but Chip wasn't interested. "Not me," he said. "I like the fresh air. I'll eat in the Yard with the Yard crew."

The Yard workers were with Chip too. He was their man! No longer could he walk the length of the Yard without a greeting: "Hi ya, Chip kid!" or "Hi ya, big-leaguer!"

Chip and Bobby were inseparable. One day Bobby showed up with a brand-new catcher's glove. "Look at me, Chip. I'm gonna be a catcher," he said confidently. "But, positively! I'll never get a chance in the outfield on this ball club, but Buster's the only catcher and if he gets hurt—" He paused and added significantly, "I hope I'll be in, but you gotta help me!"

So Chip and Bobby worked out every evening after the regular practice sessions. But not alone. Jake Miller had begun to show up at just about the same time every evening and seemed to be getting a big kick out of working his arm back in shape. "The old soupbone just needs exercise, that's all," he said, laughing.

On their way home after the Ritter game, Chip and Bobby passed by H. L. and Peggy Armstrong on their way to the gate. "Nice going, Hilton," Armstrong said. "You certainly stood them on their heads this afternoon."

"Thank you, sir."

"I want you to meet my daughter Peggy, Hilton," the boss said, smiling.

"We've already met in the cafeteria," said Chip.

Peggy turned to him with a smile, but Chip looked away.

Armstrong grasped Chip by the arm and walked with him to the exit, talking about the game, and Bobby took advantage of the opportunity to walk beside Peggy. He used the time to remind her about her poor memory about a certain lunch date with two certain guys she knew. Chip hadn't looked at Peggy and was glad when they arrived at the grandstand gate so he and Bobby could get out of there.

Kirk was waiting for Armstrong, and the two men talked over the game while Peggy thoughtfully watched the two athletes walk rapidly away.

"How's Tucker's arm, Kirk?"

"It's better, Mr. Armstrong," Kirk said cautiously. "He ought to be all right by Wednesday."

"The way Hilton is going it doesn't seem as though it will make much difference," Armstrong said cheerfully. "You'll never know how glad I am the boy is making good."

"The team has been giving the kid good support," Kirk said, "and they've been hitting behind him. I guess they were just a little slow getting started."

Armstrong smiled and then nodded thoughtfully. "Maybe you're right. Guess we'll know better on Wednesday. Hope we can take Mackin again. Who are you planning to use, Hilton or Tucker?"

"Well, I don't think Hilton will ever have as much luck against the Mackins as he did that first game, and now that Tucker's arm is coming around again, I guess I'll give him the call." Kirk watched Armstrong anxiously.

"You're sure Tucker's arm is all right now?"

"Well, he's been lookin' better all the time in practice."

Armstrong chuckled. "You don't suppose the Hilton boy's fine performance lately has had anything to do with that, do you?" he asked jokingly.

"Oh, no!" Kirk said hastily—too hastily. "Nothing like that at all. Tucker just needed a rest. He's ready! You'll see, he'll throw a good game on Wednesday."

Armstrong still seemed a little doubtful. "Well, I hope so, Kirk. Good luck."

The big man waved to his baseball manager and walked thoughtfully to his car. He climbed into the front seat where his daughter sat at the wheel.

Peggy skillfully drove her father's car toward home. "How about some golf this evening?" Armstrong asked her.

"Mother has a party planned, Dad. Don't you remember?"

"Oh, sure. What's the matter with me? Guess I was still thinking about baseball."

"Dad, what's wrong with Duck's arm?"

"Well, I don't really know, Peggy. Why?"

"Well, I saw him throwing, Dad, and he didn't throw as though he had a sore arm."

"I noticed that, too, Peggy. You see, Doctor Carter told me he couldn't find anything wrong with Tucker's arm. Said he thought it was more mental than physical."

"Mental? What did he mean?"

"I gathered he thought Tucker was faking or at least trying to alibi his pitching."

"But why, Dad? Why would Duck need an alibi? It doesn't make sense."

"I don't get it either, Peggy. Let's talk about something else. What do you think about young Hilton now?"

Peggy's answer was surprising. "I think Gunner Kirk is a rotten manager!" she said firmly.

"Kirk a rotten manager? Say, what kind of talk is that? What's that got to do with Chip Hilton's pitching?"

But Peggy Armstrong wasn't adding anything to her surprising statement. She was deep in thought. Deep in a personal problem that concerned the Steelers' pitching staff.

As the big game with the Mackins drew nearer, a feeling of expectancy backed by hopes of another victory over the league leaders gripped every Steelers player and fan. Everyone from H. L. Armstrong down was looking forward to Wednesday, July 20. If the Steelers could win, they would break their tie with the Tri-Staters and go into undisputed possession of the runner-up position. But a victory over the high and mighty Mackins, the Steelers' most bitter, most acrimonious rival, was more important than anything else.

The evening before the all-important game, Kirk and Dillon sat in the dugout watching the players' relaxed antics on the field. Dillon cleared his throat several times and then pulled a rumpled newspaper clipping from his pocket. He nudged Kirk and pointed to the headline.

"Mean anything to you?" he asked, watching Kirk intently as the manager glanced at the article. Dillon's voice was brittle with excitement, but Gunner Kirk shook his head negatively.

"No," Kirk said shortly, "nothin' at all! Why should it?"

"You mean you don't get it?" Dillon asked incredulously. He shook his head in disbelief. Dillon had an idea in his head now, and it did not seem possible that Kirk wasn't able to follow the thought.

"No, it doesn't mean nothin' to me," Kirk said impassively. "Just because the Reds are willin' to pay a hundred grand for some bush-league pitcher doesn't help me any."

"Oh, no? Look over there!" Dillon nodded toward the practice pitching rubber in front of the grandstand where Chip and Barber were playing catch.

"Look, Gunner," Dillon said eagerly, "we got us a gold mine if we play our cards right. This kid's gonna be great!"

"Where do you get that *great* stuff?" Kirk sneered. "You told me yourself the kid was a washout. How come you're changin' your mind now?"

"Well, Gunner, I gotta confess that I've been hopin' the kid was gonna turn out to be a bum, but he ain't. He's the best pitcher I ever caught right now! I hate his guts, but he's got it!"

Suddenly, as if jerked by a string, Kirk's head swung around. His sharp, black eyes were alert now as he studied Chip's free, easy delivery.

"Yeah," he mused half-aloud in a cold, calculating voice. "Yeah, you might have somethin' there, Buster. Maybe we oughta develop us a plan that involves Mr. Hilton, the high school squirt!"

CHAPTER 11

"You Said It!"

BIG NOSE proudly jammed an elbow in his companion's ribs. "Some kid, eh, Pig Iron?"

"You said it!"

Everybody was saying it! Well, everybody who worked at the Mansfield Steel Company was saying it! Chip Hilton was *some* kid! Yes sir, the kid had won five in a row, including two over the Mackins! That second game with the Steelers' industrial league rivals had been an especially sweet one! Tucker had lasted just two-thirds of an inning. With the bases full, he had been sent to the showers, and the high school star from Valley Falls had been brought in without benefit of a warm-up. Tucker's three responsibilities had watched in frustration as their next three teammates fanned the July breeze, and not another Mackin reached base during the rest of the game.

And this Saturday afternoon, Manfield's Steeler Field was jammed with Steelers fans ready to watch the kid work his magic again.

"YOU SAID IT!"

Hilton had relieved the great Tucker in the fifth when the Steelers were two runs behind and Tri-State had the bases loaded with only one man away.

And what had the kid done about *that?* Nothing much! Just struck out two men in a row to retire the side again, leaving three Tri-State ducks stranded on the pond!

"You said it!"

And then, taking Tucker's place in the batting order, the kid hadn't done much about that either, except to lift one high over the right-field fence with two aboard in the last of the seventh to put the Steelers out in front by a run.

"You said it!"

And now it was the first of the ninth with the lights of Steeler Field contending with the last bit of daylight, and the high school kid was setting the Tri-Staters down one, two, three. Then a streak of greased lightning seemed to skip from the mound to Dillon's big glove, and it was all over but the shouting! The kid had come through again!

"You said it!"

There it was! In the record! Six straight! And the Steelers were tied with the Mackins for first place!

"You said it!"

When the game was over, Steelers manager Gunner Kirk waited for H. L. Armstrong at the grandstand gate, but he was too late. The big boss had broken his pattern. Instead of waiting to talk first with Gunner Kirk, Armstrong was talking to the players in the locker room under the grandstand.

"Men, I want to congratulate you on the way you've been playing ball. I'm feeling so good about it, I think I'll send an invitation to Dave Mackin right now and invite him and his ball club to be our guests when we represent Mansfield in the national tournament this August."

He paused and glanced around at the eyes and faces of the elated players until he caught Chip's eye.

"And, Hilton, I want you to know I'm proud of your pitching. Hank Rockwell sure knew what he was talking about! I figured I could count on Rockwell. He said you'd help us out, and he was more than right! Well, boys, five to go and we're in. Let's go get them!

"I didn't come down here just to congratulate you for winning, but to let you know I have arranged a dinner and a theater outing for you and your wives or girl-friends—sorry, it's significant other now, isn't it?—for next Saturday night, July 30th. That will be right after we take the rubber game of the year from Mackin. We'll meet at the recreation building at seven o'clock. OK?"

It was OK, all right. Why wouldn't it be? H. L. Armstrong's employee parties were big-league! The enthusiastic cheer greeting Armstrong's invitation was genuine and one of the first real responses anyone in that dressing room had heard for a long time.

But one young man in that room seemed to have nothing to be happy about. Duck Tucker dressed silently with a scowl on his face. Armstrong's words of praise for wonder boy Chip Hilton had cut Tucker—cut him deeply. Last year, he had been the center of everything on this ball club, and now here was this high school nobody from out of nowhere stealing everything that should have been his. Well, the season wasn't over yet. This young superstar's luck couldn't hold out forever. August was just about the time the heat got to the rookies. Then the veteran pitchers with real talent came into their own. It wasn't over yet. Not by a long shot.

Kirk made a big deal over Chip for the first time. He slapped him on the shoulder and told him he was "really workin' now!"

"YOU SAID IT!"

Later, on the way home, Bobby echoed Armstrong's words about the national championship. "We can do it, too, Chip. If you keep going the way you're going now and they wise up to the fact that Duck Tucker is all washed up, that is."

Bobby stopped, demoralized by a sudden, sinking thought. "Hey, Chip. S'pose we did get to the nationals, would you pitch without three days' rest?"

Chip shook his head decisively. "No, I wouldn't, Bobby, much as I'd want to. But you're taking a lot for granted. The next time I pitch, I'll probably be knocked out of the box in the first inning."

Bobby was persistent. "But s'pose we did make it. You mean to tell me you wouldn't pitch after a day's rest even if it meant winning the national championship for the team and Mansfield?"

"No, I made a promise, and I intend to live up to it."

Bobby grunted. "Well, if Kirk wasn't such a stubborn, no-good guy, we'd have another good pitcher ready—Jake Miller!"

Chip went to bed early that night, tired but happy. The next morning, Mrs. Pecora was waiting for him with a newspaper and a smile on her friendly face. Chip was her star. She couldn't do enough for the teenager who was her favorite renter. She pointed a short, heavy finger at the sports section of the *Journal*.

"This one you'll like, Chip! This one you'll like!"

Chip laughed in surprise. Imagine, Mrs. Pecora reading the sports page!

"I never knew you read the sports pages, Mrs. Pecora."

"Me? I no read them! Only when you pitch the ball!" Mrs. Pecora stood by Chip's side as he read the story.

CLUTCH HITTER

STEELERS WIN SIXTH STRAIGHT
Trip Tri-State 7-6
Hilton Stars

By MIKE SHELDON

The Mansfield Steel Company's fast-stepping Steelers continued their winning ways yesterday afternoon by coming from behind to beat the Tri-Staters 7-6 before nearly 5,000 loyal spectators at Steeler Field.

Yesterday's victory was an important one for the Steelers because the Fitzgeralds upset Mackin Motors, throwing the Steelers and the Mackins into a first-place tie.

Duck Tucker started for the Steelers and was immediately in trouble. The big college hurler was wild. He got one out before Pete Bailey, who led the Tri-State attack with three hits, singled. Then Tucker passed Tommy Byrnes and retired Bob Smith only to have Bill Wolfe single in a run. Harris singled, filling the bases, and Miller doubled to right field, scoring Byrnes and Wolfe. Mark Carey flied to Lefty Curtis for the third out.

The Steelers tied it up quickly after walks to Shorty Welch and Joe Ferris and a single by Brad Cooper loaded the bases with only one out. A triple off the left-field wall by Lefty Curtis scored three.

Tri-State scored three more in the third, but the Steelers came right back and scored one in the bottom of the same frame. In the top of the fifth, Tucker got into real trouble. Carr walked, Bailey singled again, and then Tucker set Byrnes down with three pitches. But he walked Smith, loading the bases.

"YOU SAID IT!"

Steelers manager Kirk lifted Tucker at this point and sent in the league sensation, Chip Hilton. Hilton was carrying a victory string of five straight and promptly demonstrated why he is the leading pitcher in the league by striking out Bill Wolfe and Doc Harris.

In the bottom of the seventh, Lou Ferrar walked Lefty Curtis, struck out Pete Armeda, walked Catolono, and erased the hard-swinging Steelers catcher, Buster Dillon, on strikes.

Chip Hilton won his own game when he cleaned the bases by slamming a high-riding homer over the right-field wall to put the Steelers ahead 7-6 and then protected that advantage by limiting the Tri-Staters to a lone single for the two remaining frames.

The young high school star now has a consecutive victory record of six games and, while in the box, has limited his Mansfield Industrial League opponents to five runs in six games. Hilton has hit safely in the last five games.

The box score:

STEELERS	AB	R	H	BI	BB	TRI-STATE	AB	R	H	BI	BB
Welch, 2b	4	1	1	0	1	Carr, ss	4	0	0	0	1
Ferris, ss	5	1	0	0	1	Bailey, 3b	4	1	3	0	0
Murphy, cf	5	0	1	0	0	Byrnes, rf	4	1	2	0	1
Cooper, lf	4	1	3	1	0	Smith, cf	3	1	1	0	1
Curtis, 1b	4	2	2	3	1	Wolfe, 1b	4	2	1	2	0
Armeda, rf	5	0	1	0	0	Harris, lf	4	1	1	2	0
Catolono, 3b	4	1	2	0	1	Miller, 2b	4	0	1	2	0
Dillon, c	3	0	0	0	0	Carey, c	3	0	1	0	0
Tucker, p	2	0	0	0	0	Ferrar, p	3	0	0	0	0
Hilton, p	2	1	1	3	0						
Totals	38	7	11	7	4	Totals	33	6	10	6	3

TRI-STATE   303 000 000 - 6
STEELERS   301 000 30-- 7

CLUTCH HITTER

That afternoon, Chip Hilton and Bobby Barber took a walk along the tree-lined parkway that gracefully wound through Mansfield City Park. Bobby had cleverly maneuvered Chip to walk along the path that bordered the road. Chip didn't really want to walk along the road. What Chip wanted to do was walk by the lake and sit on one of the benches to watch the ducks and the two beautiful, graceful swans for a while, but Barber was being difficult.

By a strange coincidence, Peggy Armstrong and her father had been driving leisurely around that parkway at the same time. H. L. Armstrong was a little surprised by Peggy's interest in this particular stretch of the road but even more so by her unusually slow speed. Peggy was typically eager to get someplace in a hurry and had to watch her lead foot. But her father was in a good mood, and their tee time with Dave Mackin and young Dave wasn't scheduled for another hour. There was still plenty of time to dress and hit a few drives from the practice tee. So if Peggy was happy, so was he.

Strangely enough, it was Peggy who spotted Chip and Bobby. And when she pulled the big car to a stop, a little smile of discernment crossed her father's lips. So that was it!

"Hello," Peggy called. "How about a ride, gentlemen?"

H. L. Armstrong thought he knew his daughter well, but he was surprised by the tact and finesse she employed to get the two boys into the car. Hilton didn't seem too anxious to come along. It was Barber who almost forced the pitcher into the backseat.

H. L. Armstrong gave Peggy a sidelong glance and a short chuckle as she blushed, and then he gladly seconded his daughter's invitation to the two players to be their guests at the golf club that afternoon. He had looked forward with pleasure to this afternoon. And Peggy could have invited the whole baseball team to the club as far as he was concerned, just as long as he finally got there and got to keep his tee time with the Mackins. Most of his anticipated enjoyment concerned the good-natured needling he was going to give Dave Mackin over the pitching efforts of the youngster with the steady, gray eyes. And that pitcher was at that very moment sitting next to the irrepressible Bobby Barber in the backseat of his car. Having the pitcher along might just add a little more spice to the mix!

Dave Mackin and his son were H. L. Armstrong's most competitive golfing rivals. The Mackin-Armstrong foursome was always at odds about some sports rivalry, and the golf matches were usually decided on the eighteenth green.

Peggy was a steady and a reliable golfing partner. She could drive a consistent 170 yards and always scorned the women's tee. She could carry her end of the load and no help needed, thanks! H. L. hated to admit it, but it was his daughter who provided the competition that always made the match close. Peggy was always down the middle with her wood or iron, and her putting was deadly.

Young Dave, however, was as erratic as Peggy was consistent and blew up under pressure. He would hit a 250-yard drive on one tee, play a neat iron to the green, get down in two for a solid par, and, occasionally, sink one for a birdie. But on the next hole, he would try to drive 300 yards and end up in the rough and on the card with a big nine or ten (or even a seven if he wasn't watched closely).

Yes, H. L. Armstrong got a big kick out of the golf matches with the Mackins. Golf had been the only close competition for several years. Now, of course, it was a little different. The Steelers and the Mackins were tied for first place in the Mansfield Industrial Baseball Association.

"Ahem!"

"What did you say, Dad?"

"Er, nothing, Peggy. Nothing at all. I seem to have a frog in my throat."

Chip had never seen a really good golf course. There had been several miniature putt-putt courses at Valley Falls, and one or two driving ranges had tried to make a go of it. But they, like the nine-hole course that had never been much more than a field bedecked with flagsticks, had gradually gone out of business.

The Mansfield Country Club, however, was first-class. The spacious clubhouse, with its terraces, dining rooms, and locker rooms, was modern and beautiful and overlooked a superbly crafted and manicured course.

While the Armstrongs were changing into their golf clothes, Chip and Bobby lounged in the luxury of comfortable chairs on the terrace, enjoying the lush green of the tree-lined fairways set against a backdrop of deep blue skies. But Bobby couldn't sit around for too long, and the two guys left the terrace and headed over to the first tee. There, before long, Peggy, her father, Dave Mackin, and his son, Davy, joined them.

Dave Mackin was pleasant. He smiled and shook Chip's hand warmly when they were introduced. But young Mackin was abrupt and cool in his greeting. Chip was just as reserved, but Bobby hadn't forgotten the baseball razzing the younger Mackin had given Chip at a recent game and took advantage of the moment to zing a fastball at the unsuspecting Davy.

"Heard your comments in front of the bench and how

you were trying to get Chip upset last Wednesday," Bobby said disarmingly. "Didn't do you much good though," he added quickly. "Fact is, Chip never even heard you!" The short, embarrassing silence was relieved by Peggy Armstrong's musical giggle.

"Well, I heard him!" she said. "I didn't think there was anyone in Mansfield who didn't. I never heard anyone scream so loudly in my life! Or should I say cry?" She laughed, winking at Dave Mackin Sr.

Davy didn't reply, but his father accepted the challenge. "We'll see who cries the next time," he cautioned, smiling at Chip. "By the way, son, I knew your father when he was at State, so I'm not surprised that you're a great pitcher. I'm proud to know you, and I want to congratulate you on your fine pitching. Maybe we'll have a chance to get better acquainted one of these days. But right now," he glanced at H. L. with a grin, "it seems I have to give your boss another golf lesson. How about you two following along to witness the drubbing he's so deservedly going to get?"

As the foursome moved off, Chip and Bobby followed, keeping out of the way yet watching the play with interest. Bobby took time out from baseball to teach Chip something about golf. Chip soon learned to keep score and began to count each contestant's strokes. So, on the second nine, he was surprised when he heard Davy Mackin say he had taken a six on the long, par-five thirteenth hole. Chip was sure Davy had used five strokes to reach the green, and he knew positively that it had taken the cocky young golfer two to get down. That would make seven in anyone's book. He mentally reviewed Davy's strokes. A pulled drive to the rough, an iron that was also pulled and left the ball in the rough, then a dubbed stroke, a fourth iron shot that was short, and a pitch over a deep trap to the green. That had to be five, and two putts had to make it seven. Well, it was none of his business, but he was pretty sure Peggy Armstrong had noticed Davy's math problems too. She had arched her eyebrows just a little when she heard Davy calling out his score.

Bobby knew golf, all right, but baseball was his thing. He was tired of the game now, and his remarks were pointed and sharp. "Golf's for old men," he said disdainfully.

Chip laughed. "How about young women?" he asked, watching Bobby closely.

Bobby's eyes shot toward Peggy Armstrong. "Oh, yeah," he said, "I see what you mean, but that's different!" He sighed and added, "Plenty different!"

Chip knew exactly what Bobby Barber meant.

CHAPTER 12

Ideals Are Not for Sale

BUGS KIERAN, the Steelers' publicity man, looked up from his camera and gently cajoled, "Come on, guys. Let's get this over! Hold it just a second!"

Buster Dillon had surprised Chip and everyone else by moving close to the kid's side and throwing a heavy arm over the slender hurler's shoulder. "I," he insisted loudly, "wanna have my picture taken beside my battery mate!"

Chip was flabbergasted. It was the first open gesture of friendship the boisterous catcher had ever made, and Chip suspected some sort of joke. But it seemed there was no catch to it this time. Buster's bearlike hug was warm and his grin was wide, so Chip returned the burly receiver's smile.

"All right, now, hold it!" Kieran urged. "Let's have a big smile." Kieran snapped the camera. "OK, that's it!"

The Steelers broke ranks and trotted out on the field. Anyone who had seen this ball club four weeks earlier would have doubted that the personnel could be the

CLUTCH HITTER

same. A winning club is a happy club and this one was no exception, except for one person—the Steelers' star college hurler, Duck Tucker. Kirk had nominated Tucker for the pitching honors against the Fitzgerald Painters, and now Tucker was walking slowly to the mound.

Tucker's mind was a seething mixture of jealousy, bitterness, anger, and contempt. He was in no mood to pitch, and the fans' evident disappointment when he, and not Chip Hilton, arrived at the mound was like pouring salt in his already painfully wounded, overinflated ego.

"We want the kid!"

"What's the matter with Hilton?"

"Put a real pitcher in there, Kirk!"

"Back to college, Tucker! We want Hilton!"

By the time the umpire had called "Play ball," Tucker was in a murderous mood. He pitched with every bit of his usual skill, but nothing clicked. It was one of those nightmares of a game when an easy infield out turns into a hit because of a bad bounce; a strikeout is lost because of a missed ball; a bunt outside the baseline spins fair just as it is about to be trapped in foul territory; and a missed sign leads to a costly, errant throw. One team plays perfect ball, the other can do nothing right.

The Painters took full advantage of the breaks and scored twice in the first inning. And just to keep up that inexplicable series of events that baseball players call the breaks of the game, every ball the Steelers hit homed directly into a Fitzgerald fielder's hands. That's the way the game continued until Tucker was a nervous mess. He had just about reached the breaking point. In the top of the sixth with the Fitzgeralds leading 6-1 and Painters on first and second with one down, Lefty Curtis, the Steelers' lanky first baseman, gave Dillon the sign for the pickoff play at first.

IDEALS ARE NOT FOR SALE

But Buster, who had been watching the long lead the Painter on second base had taken toward third, absent-mindedly gave Tucker the sign for a pickoff throw to second base.

Tucker counted three, whirled, and whipped the ball to second base. But the only person who dashed madly for the bag was the Fitzgerald runner. He saw Tucker pivot and saw that he was caught. So he hit the dirt, expecting the tag. Then he saw that the bag was uncovered, the ball was bouncing its way to center field. He scrambled to his feet and dashed for third base. Shorty Welch and Joe Ferris had been caught flat-footed. Shorty caught Dillon's sign too late, and Matt Murphy, out in center field, had been taken by surprise too. But he tried, too hard and too late, and the grass cutter skidded under his glove and out to the fence.

Both runners tallied to make the score 8-1. And that set off the fireworks. Tucker raised his glove high over his head and threw it to the ground with all his power. Then he charged wildly out to second base angrily berating Welch and Ferris. Lefty Curtis tried to explain that the play was at first and not at second, and Tucker turned on him. Then Buster lumbered out. Tucker shook his fist under Dillon's nose, shoved him, and called him a blockhead. It was a circus! At that, Tucker stalked off the field, shaking his head and angrily blaming every player on the team for his bad luck.

Kirk met him at the third-base line, after calling time.

"Where do you think you're going? Get back in there! What's the matter with you? You don't ever leave the field unless I say so!"

But Tucker was through. He had lost all self-control. He pushed Kirk roughly aside and continued to the dugout, accompanied by the jeers and taunts of every person in the park. Kirk was furious, too, and followed Tucker clear into the dugout, trying to coax him back onto the field. But it was no use. In the end, it was Chip Hilton who walked slowly out to the mound to receive a tremendous ovation from the Steelers supporters.

"Never too late, kid!"

"We're with you, Hilton!"

"Game's not over! Pour it on 'em, kid!"

But Chip didn't have to pour it on. It seemed the whole complexion of the game changed and shifted with his first pitch. Now the Steelers could do no wrong, and the Painters could do nothing right. In that same inning, in the Steelers' half of the frame, they batted around and took the lead, 9-8. And they held the score right there to rack up the Steelers and Chip Hilton's seventh-straight win. Chip went two for two at the plate.

After the game, Kirk and Dillon drove slowly away from the field in the manager's car. Buster was boiling.

"I'm not gonna take much more from that guy, Gunner," he growled. "I don't know why I didn't bust him this afternoon! Who does he think he is?"

Kirk was in deep thought. "I know, I know," he said impatiently. "I'm about fed up too. I wish I could drop him from the Sunday deal. If I could only get a hold of another pitcher."

"What about the kid?"

"I don't wanna spoil the contract deal we've got cooked up, but if we could maneuver him into the Sunday money games, it might help us a lot in the other plan too. I'd like to sound him out before comin' right out and askin' him."

"Well, why don't you?"

"Too dangerous! Maybe, though, if we both got him away somewhere, we could sorta feel him out—see if he'd go for it. Let's ask him to go out to the Silver Slipper to-morrow night, OK?"

They rode in silence for a short distance, and then Kirk slowed the car and continued. "Look, Buster, we gotta play it safe. You proposition him and if he goes along, OK. If he bucks, I'll step in and get you off the hook so he won't think we were tryin' to maneuver him. Get it?"

Buster Dillon grunted his agreement, and the two men were silent the rest of the way home.

Chip was surprised at the invitation he received the following evening at practice. Why, sure he'd go out that night! No, he'd never been to the Silver Slipper. He'd heard about it though. Yes, he'd be ready about nine o'-clock when Kirk drove around to Mrs. Pecora's.

Chip had never been to a nightclub before in his life. He'd seen them portrayed in the movies a couple of times, and he had enjoyed the music, the lighting, the decorations, and the colorful people. The name, the Silver Slipper, sounded kind of interesting to him, but when Chip, Kirk, and Dillon were ushered into the dimly lighted, noisy, smoke-filled hall, Chip was keenly disappointed.

A long bar on one side of the room was crowded with mostly men and a few women seated on high stools. In front of the bar, and stretching to the opposite wall, ta-bles were packed so closely together that there didn't seem any way for people to leave once they were seated. In the rear of the barnlike room, there was a small dance floor and beyond that a stage. On the stage a five-member local band was playing its version of current hits. The group was primed for the crowd and obviously had a following, judging by the crowded dance floor. Chip couldn't figure how people could move, much less dance on that small, packed area. At least Bobby wasn't there to try to get him out on the dance floor this time.

A bored waiter in an overworn tux a few sizes too small in the jacket and about two sizes too big in the slacks led them to a corner table and, unconsciously hitching up his pants, informed them there was a special comedy show at ten o'clock. In a monotone voice reflecting his lack of interest, he asked the men what they wanted to drink. Kirk and Dillon ordered drafts and Chip asked for a Diet Coke. Chip looked around at the crowd, watched the dancers, and thought to himself, *The fashion police have never been in this place.* Many of the couples were talking and laughing as they danced. They seemed to have no difficulty maneuvering through the crowd. Others were clumsy, bumping into everyone on the floor at one time or another.

The comedy show was about the same caliber as the rest of the Silver Slipper, definitely in keeping with the surroundings. Inexperienced as Chip was, he quickly sensed the show was cheap, tawdry, and in bad taste. It wasn't even as good as the small-time, amateur stand-up comics who sometimes appeared at the high school talent show in Valley Falls. He was glad when it was over. So were Kirk and Dillon. They were anxious to get on with their plans.

Deliberately, but not very cleverly, they led the conversation to Chip and his home and ambitions. He told them about his college dreams, his father's death, his mother's supervisory position with the phone company, and his determination to finance his own way through school by working.

"Look, anyone who can throw like you can, kid, don't have to worry none about finances," Dillon said knowingly. "Why, Duck Tucker's paid his way just on his Sunday pitchin' alone!"

IDEALS ARE NOT FOR SALE

"Sunday pitching?"

"Sure! Tucker pitches Sunday baseball from May first to the last of September. All the college guys do it! Duck makes better'n two thousand dollars. Just throwin' on Sundays—"

Kirk interrupted. "But they play under assumed names, Chip. Why, half the athletes playin' that kind of baseball are college guys, but no one ever says anything about it or even cares about it."

"But that makes them professionals!"

Dillon laughed boisterously. "So? Nobody cares about that. There's hundreds of college guys playin' and makin' that easy money. Some guys, the real good ones, just pitch on the weekends. That's their whole job for the summer."

Chip was bewildered. "That's hard to believe," he said in a shocked voice. "I'm sorry, but I've never heard about anything like this before."

"You oughtn't to pass up all that easy money," Dillon said earnestly. "Nobody'd ever be the wiser."

"I wouldn't do it if I never got through college," Chip said determinedly. "I'd rather work my way through with a pick and shovel." He laughed. "Guess I'll have to do that anyway."

"I don't see what you're worryin' about," Buster argued. "Tucker's been doin' it for years. Why, he's pitchin' every Sunday right now! You know how much he makes on a good Sunday? If he wins? No? Well, he nearly makes more in one afternoon playin' baseball than you make in a week in the Yard, wrestlin' with steel!"

Dillon paused to let that sink in and then continued. "And you're a *better* pitcher than Tucker, Chip." Dillon leaned closer across the table at Chip and lowered his voice, "Man, you could rack up five hundred to a thousand bucks with no trouble at all between now and fall. What d'ya say? Wanna give it a whirl?"

Chip shook his head grimly. "No, sir! Not me! I don't need money *that* bad! I don't understand it."

Kirk and Dillon knew when they were whipped. Their eyes met and they called off their scheme. The high school squirt had ideals and they weren't for sale. As he said he would, Kirk tried to ease them out of the situation.

"You know, Chip," the manager said smoothly, "you're right! I'm sure glad to see you stick by your principles. We're glad you're that kinda guy. There ain't many guys around like you anymore. I want you to understand that Buster, here, didn't have no ulterior motive. There's so many so-called amateurs playin' baseball and makin' money at it that it isn't even funny. Buster just wanted to help you out. Forget all about it!"

Dillon yawned. "Gettin' late," he said. "We ought to hit the road. Another tough day tomorrow at the mill, especially for you guys in the Yard."

Kirk and Dillon were not quite so upbeat on the trip home. Chip was puzzled by all the information he'd learned that night and was trying to figure out what it was all about as he sat quietly in the front seat. Duck Tucker pitching every Sunday for money, and he'd been doing it all the way through college? It just didn't make sense. He didn't know whether to believe it or not.

After Kirk and Dillon dropped Chip off at Mrs. Pecora's, they continued on to one of their favorite late-night spots and took a booth in the rear of the room, out of earshot of the other late customers.

"Well, looks like we rushed him a bit," Dillon said moodily.

"Yeah," Kirk assented, "we messed up that one! But good!"

IDEALS ARE NOT FOR SALE

Dillon was deep in thought, his face furrowed by a scowl. After a brief silence, he shook his head doubtfully. "I don't think the other thing's gonna work either," he said in a discouraged tone.

"You mean about tryin' to get his name on some contract deal?"

"Yeah!"

"Well, that's a little different. You see, he's a minor and a contract wouldn't hold up legally anyway, but I was thinkin' it might give us a sort of moral hold on him. See? He's square, all right, and if we could get his name on a contract with the understandin' that it would be kept quiet, he'd probably stick by it, minor or no minor."

Dillon shook his head. "Nope," he said, "it won't work! Not for a couple thousand bucks, it won't. Now, if it was twenty or thirty grand or some big amount like that, it might. Still, I don't know. He's a stubborn kid."

Kirk nodded grimly. "He's stubborn, all right. And I don't believe any amount of money would buy him off. He probably knows the big leagues can't sign up a minor until he's through high school and maybe he knows signin' a contract would make him ineligible for anymore playin' in high school and college. He's dead set on that school stuff. Maybe you're right. Maybe we ought to work some kind of a trick deal. Start thinkin' about it."

Chip had difficulty getting to sleep that night. He couldn't fit all the pieces of the jigsaw puzzle together no matter how he tried, and he found it hard to believe all the things he had been told about Tucker. No wonder Tucker had looked so bad on the mound. He'd evidently been pitching too much and in too many places. Man, if Buster had been telling the truth, Tucker had been pitching even while he was playing for the university! That was no good! If the university ever found out about that, Tucker could be in trouble.

He couldn't help wondering about Gunner Kirk and Buster Dillon too. What was behind their sudden interest in a friendship with Chip Hilton? Probably nothing at all. Still, they were pretty tricky individuals. Chip's last thought as he nodded off to sleep was that he'd better be careful around those two, all the time.

CHAPTER 13

Freedom of the Press

MIKE SHELDON was one of the best newspaper men in the state, and he'd rather write about baseball than eat or sleep. The surprise winning streak of the Steelers had given him a lot to write about during the past month, and today he figured he'd get two birds with one stone: cover the Mackin-Steeler game for his Sunday story and write a feature article on Chip Hilton for his Tuesday column. He cast a pleased look at the sunny, blue sky and sighed with satisfaction. It was a great day for a baseball game. When he arrived at the ballpark, he saw Chip and Bobby Barber playing catch in front of the Steelers dugout. He strolled in that direction, stopping to chat briefly with Gunner Kirk on the way.

Chip figured he might get the chance to pitch against the Mackins today, and he had started an early warm-up. As he gradually increased the power behind his throws, he kept puzzling over what Kirk and Dillon had told him last night. He could understand now why Tucker didn't want to pitch the Saturday games and why he had seemed pleased when Chip got the call to work. Chip wondered if Tucker had been faking about his sore arm too. Chip had a hunch Duck Tucker wouldn't pitch today either. That meant Chip Hilton would get the call. Good! He was ready.

"Hello, Hilton."

Chip turned to see a tall, slender man, wearing glasses and smiling at him with friendly ease. He smiled briefly in return, but there was a questioning look in his eyes. He had never seen this man before.

"Hi, my name is Mike Sheldon. I write for the *Journal*."

"Oh, I'm glad to meet you, Mr. Sheldon. I read your column all the time."

Chip knew who Mike Sheldon was, all right. Anyone who was interested in sports in the state knew who Sheldon was, knew he was regarded as the best sportswriter in the state and one of the best in the country. Chip looked carefully at this writer. He'd heard a lot about Sheldon and he'd read most of his articles too. Someday, maybe, if things went right, he'd be a sportswriter like Mike Sheldon.

"Hope you don't mind me barging in on you like this, Hilton. I asked Gunner if I could take a little of your practice time. I want to do a story on you." Sheldon paused and a brief smile crossed his lips as he continued. "You've been making a lot of news around here lately, and my boss thought maybe I ought to see what makes you tick."

Chip wasn't too enthusiastic about Sheldon's proposition, but he waited silently for Sheldon to continue.

"S'pose we sit over here in the bleachers where we won't be disturbed."

FREEDOM OF THE PRESS

Chip was slightly confused, but he tossed the ball to Bobby, asked him to excuse him for a minute, and followed Sheldon to a seat in the first row of the bleachers. Sheldon pulled a small, green notebook out of his pocket, and he tapped it rhythmically with a pencil as he talked.

"I've never actually been down to Valley Falls, Hilton, but I feel almost as though I know you. Mind if I call you Chip?" He continued without waiting for Chip's response. "Even though we've never met before, Chip, I've covered dozens of the football, basketball, and baseball games you played in, so I guess through my writing we could say we're acquainted. You've made quite a reputation for yourself, Chip. A fine one!"

Chip was embarrassed by Sheldon's remarks, but there was nothing he could do or say except sit there and take it. The feeling wore away, however, during the next few minutes, and when Sheldon closed his notebook and slipped it in his coat pocket, Chip felt as though he had known the slender writer all his life. Guess that's part of the reason he's so good at what he does, Chip mused. He makes a guy feel comfortable talking to him.

While Chip and Sheldon were talking in the bleachers, the other members of the team were covertly watching the two with mixed emotions. Sheldon was well-known to every player there. Three people were particularly observant.

Gunner Kirk was disgusted. He didn't want Chip to get too much publicity, and he didn't want Sheldon to get too interested in Chip Hilton. "Oughta know better'n come out here right before a game," he grouched. "As if the kid hasn't had too much publicity already."

Buster Dillon wondered what Sheldon's appearance was all about and wandered over beside Kirk. "That kid's startin' to get a lot of publicity, Gunner. We better work fast if we're gonna pull this off!"

Duck Tucker was in a jealous sulk and could barely restrain himself as Chip and Sheldon walked slowly along the third-base line and by the dugout. *"Everybody falls for that jerk's line,"* he muttered. "Hope he gets his ears pinned back today."

Sheldon paused in front of the dugout, and his words were clearly heard by everyone near the Steelers bench. "The story will be in Tuesday's paper, Hilton," he said. "Watch for it! I hope you like it, fella!"

City Stadium was jammed. An overflow crowd lined the baselines from first and third bases clear out to the fence. Local fans had never seen a crowd this big! The Steelers and Mackins were tied for first place, and a victory today for either team would just about clinch the title and the right to represent Mansfield in the national championship tournament.

Big Nose and Pig Iron had managed to get their favorite seats on the third-base line, and their iron-lunged shouts carried clearly above the bedlam of cheers, jeers, catcalls, boos, and applause.

While the teams were taking fielding and hitting practice, both managers were warming up their key pitchers. Chip and Tucker were throwing to Dillon, standing as far apart as the practice rubber permitted and ignoring each other completely. Bobby sat in front of the dugout with his new catching glove, waiting for Buster Dillon to take his position at the plate when infield practice started. Bobby wanted to warm up Chip and pep him up a bit too.

Kirk walked up behind Chip and Tucker and talked quietly to the two pitchers. "How you feelin' today, Duck?" he asked softly. "Is the arm OK?"

FREEDOM OF THE PRESS

Tucker checked his windup and shook his head half-heartedly. "Not too good, Gunner. I'll go, though, if you just say the word."

"How about you, Hilton?"

"I feel great, Mr. Kirk. Great!"

"OK, Hilton, you go!"

In front of the other dugout, Red Corrigan, the Mackins' tall, right-handed speed merchant, and Lefty Kurt, the tricky southpaw, were casually warming up. Between throws, they cast curious glances at Hilton and Tucker.

Steelers fans were on the beam and wired! This was the game to win! If only that guy Kirk would quit trying to engineer everything and just use the kid, everything would be all right. The kid would do it if he got any kind of support and a couple of runs. Good support was the most important thing! The kid would go get his own runs if he had to. Wasn't he leading the team in hitting and hadn't he won his own game in four of the seven he had chalked up?

If the Steelers won this one, they'd be sitting pretty! One game out in front and only three more to play: Tri-State, Fitzgerald Paints, and Ritter Automotive. It would be a cinch!

Two hours later, Mike Sheldon snapped the cover on his laptop and started for the *Journal* sports office. "Another day, another story," he murmured. "Now for a nice, quiet Sunday at home."

At the *Journal* with his feet up on his desk, Sheldon reread his story of the game.

CLUTCH HITTER

STEELERS WIN KEY GAME
MACKINS SHUT OUT
Hilton Boss on Hill with No-Hitter
CORRIGAN TIGHTENS TOO LATE

Those amazing Steelers and their even more amazing young hurler, William "Chip" Hilton, collared Mackin Motors yesterday afternoon at City Stadium in front of a boisterous 5,297 spectators. Even before the young Valley Falls All-State hurler had thrown his blinding slider past Ed Jansen for the final strike of the game, a cheering crowd of Steelers rooters were on the field milling around the young star.

Hilton was in command all the way. In the bottom of the first frame, he gave observing fans a taste of what was to come when he struck out the first three men to face him. After that, he continued the whitewash fever for eight innings and the game. The splendid pitcher from Valley Falls was never in trouble. Sharp fielding by the hustling Steelers helped Hilton out in hurling the first no-hit game in the history of the league.

The favored Mackin Motors never gave up and never stopped trying, but it was just no go. The Steelers, boasting a seven-game winning streak, played near-perfect ball to apply the white coat to their hitter opponents.

Red Corrigan got by the first two innings but ran into trouble in the third. With two down, Catolono on third, and Dillon on second base, Corrigan concentrated on Hilton, working the count to two and two. Then Hilton, who throws right-handed and bats left-handed, passed up a low inside curve, and the count

FREEDOM OF THE PRESS

was three and two. Corrigan tried a fastball, and Hilton pulled a sharp hit along the first-base foul line and played it safe. Catolono and Dillon scored. That ended the scoring for both clubs. Corrigan got Welch on a sharp grounder, then throttled the Steelers the rest of the way.

The Steelers' victory puts them in a commanding position for the league championship since they have only three games left to play, one each with Tri-State, Fitzgerald, and Ritter. The Mackins, however, must play a double bill with Fitzgerald, one game with Tri-State, and make up a postponed game with Ritter Automotive.

The box score:

MANSFIELD STEEL	AB	R	H	BI	BB		MACKIN MOTORS	AB	R	H	BI	BB
Welch, 2b	4	0	0	0	0		Sharp, rf	3	0	0	0	1
Ferris, ss	4	0	0	0	0		Jones, ss	4	0	0	0	0
Murphy, cf	3	0	0	0	1		Rice, cf	3	0	0	0	0
Cooper, lf	4	0	2	0	0		Lemler, lf	3	0	0	0	0
Curtis, 1b	4	0	1	0	0		Wilson, 3b	3	0	0	0	0
Armeda, rf	2	0	0	0	1		Bensinger, 2b	3	0	0	0	0
Catolono, 3b	3	1	1	0	0		Gallagher, 1b	3	0	0	0	0
Dillon, c	3	1	1	0	0		Houghton, c	2	0	0	0	1
Hilton, p	3	0	1	2	0		Corrigan, p	3	0	0	0	0
Totals	30	2	6	2	2		Totals	27	0	0	0	2

MANSFIELD STEEL   002 000 000 -- 2
MACKIN MOTORS   000 000 000 -- 0

Sheldon sighed with relief and tossed the computer-generated sheets in the outgoing basket. Then his eyes fell on the envelope containing the letter he'd been thinking about all day long. He had read that letter earlier in the day and had wanted to destroy it, but something re-strained him. With a reluctant gesture, he picked up the envelope and slowly removed the typewritten letter.

Mike Sheldon had the knack of ferreting out a sports story, and once equipped with the details, he could de-velop it into a real news scoop. But one of the unavoid-able nuisances of the writing profession particularly an-noyed Sheldon: he despised anonymous letters.

With an impulsive movement, he wadded the sheet of paper and made a neat two-pointer into the recycling bin. Then he scooped up his briefcase and laptop and started home. At the door, he stopped and looked back. He had a hunch about that letter. Of course, it was rumor stuff, but still he had a hunch.

Walking slowly back to his desk, he sighed wearily, then dug the letter from the bin. Smoothing out the crumpled sheet of paper, he carefully read the type-written page again.

July 29

Mike Sheldon
Sports Department
The Journal

Dear Mike:

Want a story that will splash every sports page in the state? If so, drive over to Glendale this coming Sunday afternoon. There will be a dilly of a semipro ball game at Brock Field between Glendale and Mercer and you'll get a big kick and a big-ger story out of the Glendale battery.

A fan who likes clean amateur sports

P.S. Be sure to bring a camera.

FREEDOM OF THE PRESS

Sheldon read the anonymous letter again, and then dug into the bin for the envelope the letter had arrived in. He found it and studied the postmark carefully. The letter had been mailed from Mansfield on July 29, but the envelope contained no other identification; Mike's name and address had been typed on the same machine as the letter.

Sheldon hooked his thumbs in his belt and leaned back in the chair. Through the years he had received thousands of unsigned letters and anonymous telephone tips. He disliked rumor writing and newspaper reporters who used unconfirmed gossip in their columns. His thoughts flew back to his early days as a cub reporter. It had been a struggle to make ends meet, to get enough lines in print and bylines just to keep up with his rent.

In one of those early days, he had heard some gossip that made a dynamite story. He wrote the story and was delighted when the editor patted him on the back and showered him with compliments. Later, however, a hurried call from the copy desk sent him scurrying back to meet the editor's query, "Did you confirm this story, Mike?"

"Why . . . why, no, sir," Sheldon had stuttered. "If I had, sir . . . er . . . there wouldn't have been a story!"

The editor meticulously tore the typewritten pages into minute bits while Mike watched him in amazement. He'd just been complimented on that story! What had happened to change the editor's mind? That had been quickly cleared up for him.

"This is a rumor story, Mike. An unsubstantiated fantasy of someone's mind they want us to print. You know, Mike, the *New York Times* is one of the world's greatest papers. Do you know the slogan that appears on its masthead? It's a good one for you to remember, to memorize right now: 'All the news that's fit to print!'"

CLUTCH HITTER

The editor's stern lecture that followed destroyed much of young Mike Sheldon's reporting naiveté, and he had never written another rumor story. But Mike Sheldon was first, last, and all the time a newspaper reporter, and he had never passed up the opportunity to check out a lead if it held promise of a scoop. But he always verified it and confirmed any information before writing any article.

So it was not surprising that Sunday afternoon found Mike Sheldon sitting in the stands at Brock Field in Glendale. He was located in exactly the right spot for the story he wrote and for the picture his photographer had snapped, which was to supplement and substantiate the featured story in the *Mansfield Journal's* sports section, Tuesday morning, August 2.

CHAPTER 14

Mike Sheldon's Story

CHIP HILTON could scarcely believe his eyes. No way! This must be a joke, one of those fake newspapers. He glanced at the picture at the top of the sports page and then reread the headline.

Then he looked up in the corner for the date. There it was, Tuesday morning, August 2. His shocked eyes flashed to Bobby's sober face and back to the picture for verification.

It was Tucker, all right! And Buster Dillon too! Both in Glendale uniforms!

So it had all been true. Gunner Kirk and Buster Dillon hadn't been kidding about Tucker. No wonder they'd been so sure. Dillon was in on it too!

CLUTCH HITTER

STAR STEELERS HURLER EXPOSED AS PROFESSIONAL
Play-for-Pay Athlete No Amateur
A *Journal* Exclusive

BY MIKE SHELDON

Richard "Duck" Tucker, star State hurler and one of the Mansfield Steelers' pitching aces, pitched for the Glendale Bears last Sunday in a game against the Mercer Tigers. A *Journal* photographer snapped a picture (shown above) of the game with Tucker and Buster Dillon, the Steelers' regular catcher, in Glendale uniforms.

Investigation disclosed that this was not the first game Tucker and Dillon have played for Glendale. Tucker, under the name of Tyler, and Dillon, representing himself as Duncan, have regularly appeared in Glendale uniforms for the past two months.

The explosion that is sure to follow this exposure will rock the Mansfield Industrial Amateur Baseball League to its foundation. The league rules state that any player, or players, who participate in a game and receive payment are considered professional, and they and their team or teams shall be subject to indefinite suspension and all games won shall be forfeited to its opponents.

It is understood that a league meeting will be held this evening.

The suspension will automatically eliminate the Steelers from consideration for participation in the National Amateur Tournament. The following excerpt clearly indicates the position of the national association with respect to eligibility:

"Any club that violates any of the eligibility provisions will be dropped immediately from further competition, and all games previously played shall be declared forfeited. Reinstatement of the individual implicated in the violation and of the team of which he is a member will be at the discretion of the local commission of the area affected."

Mackin Motors will benefit most by the suspension since the three defeats suffered at the hands of the Steelers will be chalked up in the victory column, making it necessary for the Mackins to win only one more game to clinch the Mansfield championship.

Chip was stunned. "Wow!" he said lamely, "What a mess!"

"I'll say!" Bobby returned. "Man, oh, man! Everbody in the Yard's up in the air. They don't know what to think, but they're plenty mad about what this does to the Steelers and our chances to play in the national tournament."

"What's going to happen now?" Chip asked anxiously.

Bobby Barber's usually gleaming blue eyes were discouraged and dull like the sea on an overcast day. "Armstrong will probably explode. I wouldn't want to be in Duck Tucker's shoes. Buster Dillon's either, for that matter."

Bobby was right about H. L. Armstrong. The president of the Mansfield Steel Company was on a rampage. The Yard grapevine, hooked into the secretarial staff in the main offices, worked double overtime all morning with reports of the comings and goings in Armstrong's office. Duck Tucker and Buster Dillon had been in Armstrong's office for two hours. Then, at 11:30, Gunner Kirk had stamped out of the recreation office after being summoned to H. L. Armstrong's office to join the meeting.

CLUTCH HITTER

The lunch hour that day was unusually quiet. The only subject of conversation was the *Journal* story. Many of the more aggressive employees were openly abusive in their references to Mike Sheldon. Others were bitterly resentful toward Tucker and Dillon. All the workers were dejected because of the disaster that had blasted the Steelers' baseball hopes. It was a cruel blow to the entire team.

At two o'clock, the news everyone had been expecting flashed through the Yard. Tucker and Dillon had been fired. Tucker had implicated Kirk, and Armstrong had fired the manager too. Baseball was out for the rest of the summer, maybe forever. All members of the baseball team were to report to Steeler Field at 4:30.

The minutes dragged for Chip that long Tuesday afternoon. His heart was heavy. Everything had been going so well. The Saturday night celebration following the Mackin shutout had been one long to remember. After church on Sunday, Chip had been invited to Jake Miller's house. Bert Long, Bobby, and Chip had joined Jake and his wife and their three kids for a barbecue and a swim in the pool in their backyard. But he had liked Monday best of all. He was met with a friendly greeting or a slap on the back at every turn.

And now that was all over. All the hopes for the city championship and for the right to play in the national championships were gone. It just didn't seem possible. Gone forever, as far as Chip Hilton was concerned.

But it was possible, and all too true. At 4:30, H. L. Armstrong faced the players in the dressing room under the grandstand.

"Men," Armstrong said quietly, "I guess you know what this meeting is all about. I know you must have seen the story in this morning's *Journal* and must realize what it means to you, to your teammates, to your fellow employees, and to me."

He sighed deeply. After a few seconds he continued. "It's pretty hard to take, but it's true—and—well, it looks as though we'll have to drop baseball for a year or so. I talked to Tucker and Dillon today and they've admitted everything.

"Furthermore, Tucker implicated Gunner Kirk, and naturally I couldn't keep them here after this, so I've dropped all three from the company payroll and the team effective immediately."

It was a disheartened squad of baseball players who checked in their equipment after Armstrong's departure. There just wasn't anything to say, and one by one, they quietly left the dressing room.

Chip and Bobby spent the rest of that afternoon and evening sitting on a bench by the lake in the park. Neither felt like eating anything, and it was quite dark and well after nine o'clock before they called it a day.

While Chip and Bobby had been sitting glumly in the park, Duck Tucker had been busy at some of the pool-rooms and other Steelers hangouts trying to talk himself out of his predicament. He was big into damage control. He had to keep up his image—all style and no substance.

"Chip Hilton was at the bottom of the whole deal. Just because he wanted to be the whole show—"

"That Hilton must have snitched! Couldn't be anybody else! Every player on the team saw him talking to Mike Sheldon before the Mackin game. They all heard Sheldon tell Hilton to watch Tuesday's paper—"

Gunner Kirk and Buster Dillon didn't help Chip either. They were also blaming him for the newspaper story and the loss of their jobs. They knew their plan to trick Chip into a baseball contract was wrecked now. They were also still bitter because they hadn't been able to get Chip to play money ball, so they attacked him openly, telling anybody who'd listen—and plenty did—that the high school squirt had spilled the whole thing to Sheldon.

Angry murmurs spread through the plant the next day. Chip noticed a sudden coolness toward him by some of the men who'd been friendly and had backed him in pitching, but he figured it was only a natural reaction to the shattered baseball hopes of the Yard. He knew everybody was down, just as he was.

But Bert Long, Jake Miller, and Bobby Barber knew better. They knew what was going on with Duck Tucker and his phony alibis. They knew what he'd been saying and they knew the effect his stories were having on his interested listeners.

Without Hilton even knowing what was happening, they rallied to Chip's support, ridiculing Tucker's cheap efforts to peg the blame on some other guy for his own downfall. When Bert, Jake, and Bobby were told that Kirk and Dillon had pointed at Chip as the one who'd tipped off Sheldon about the story, they asked for proof.

"Kirk and Dillon had told Hilton about Tucker!"

"So what? That didn't necessarily mean that Chip told Sheldon. What did he have to gain? He's not that kind of guy!"

Despite their efforts, however, the story that the kid had snitched on Tucker and Dillon and was responsible for ruining everything for the team spread through the Yard and finally through the whole plant.

It wasn't that the Yard condoned the use of illegal tactics or ineligible players. That was out! Tucker, Dillon, and Kirk had got what they deserved! But the Yard despised a squealer. That sort of a sneak was the lowest of lows—beneath contempt. So Chip Hilton got the silent treatment. It was gradual at first, scarcely noticeable. But soon the absence of the usual hellos, the averted glances, and the turned heads began to register. Bobby, Jake Miller, and Bert Long fought the treatment all the way and tried to shield Chip from its effects, but it was too apparent. Chip was shut out and receiving the chill. Arctic blasts in the dead of summer.

Now Chip was really angry. This was too much. He'd given his co-workers everything he had, and then they turned on him and unjustly blamed him for something he knew nothing about. All right, if that was the way they wanted it, they could have it that way. But two things were sure! He wasn't going to be run out of the Yard because of the silent treatment, and he was going to find out who *was* responsible for that story! And he was going to start finding that out tonight!

Bobby was waiting when the four o'clock siren wailed. Matching strides and bitterly conscious of the silent treatment, they made the long walk together through the Yard. Each time someone averted his eyes or turned his head, Bobby would mutter, "The same back at ya, buddy!" or "You too!"

But his friend's mumbling made no impression on Chip. He was concentrating on his plan of action. Mike Sheldon had acted like a nice, solid guy and had seemed friendly. Well, he would soon know if his impression was accurate.

Bobby was having a hard time trying to keep up with Chip's long stride through the Yard. Once outside the main gate, he slackened the pace. But Chip wasn't slowing down; he was in a hurry and had a destination in mind.

"Hey, where you going? What's the rush?" Barber complained.

"To see Mike Sheldon!"

"You're going to punch Sheldon in the nose, I hope, I hope!"

Chip was brief in his answer. "No," he said shortly. "I'm not going to punch Sheldon in the nose! At least, not unless he punches me first a few times!"

"Chip, if you're set on doing this tonight, we'll have to take the bus. My car's still in the shop. If you plan to walk all the way, I'll see you in the Yard tomorrow," Bobby laughed.

Fairview was seven miles from Mansfield and the bus stopped at every corner, or it sure seemed that way to the impatient Chip and Bobby. It was ten o'clock when they reached the little town and 10:30 before they found where Mike Sheldon, the sportswriter, lived. But there wasn't a light on in Sheldon's house.

Bobby was disgusted and tired. "Now what?" he demanded.

Chip was disappointed. At the *Journal* office in Mansfield, they had been told that Mike Sheldon had left long ago, that he was planning to attend a banquet at the Athletic Club at eight o'clock. But Mike Sheldon didn't show up for the banquet, and when Chip and Bobby went back to the *Journal* building, someone in the sports office—again irritated by Chip and Bobby's interruptions—said Sheldon was probably at home where he'd be if he wasn't working late at the paper.

Yes, Sheldon had a phone, but his number was unlisted. No, he didn't know the number and he wouldn't give it to them if he did.

The guy lived out in Fairview someplace, and what was so important that it couldn't wait until morning?

Chip looked again at Mike Sheldon's darkened house and sighed. They'd been on a wild goose chase all evening trying to find Mike Sheldon. Now, here they were all the way out here for nothing. Then his hopes brightened. Maybe Mr. and Mrs. Sheldon were at a movie or out to dinner.

"We'll wait!" he said decisively, sitting down on the steps.

"Oh, no. Come on, Chip. Let's head on home. We gotta work tomorrow. We can catch him tomorrow."

"No, we'll wait!"

Chip hesitated. A clock somewhere slowly struck eleven. When the last note had died away, Chip leaped to his feet and determinedly started up the steps to the porch.

"Where you going? What you gonna do?"

"I'm going to ring that doorbell right now! We'll find out right now whether he's home or not!"

Mike Sheldon was half-asleep, but he recognized the two boys immediately. He knew instantly the reason for their visit, and he was careful not to unlatch the screen door. Athletes and sports fans sometimes took exception to a writer's interpretation of "freedom of the press."

"Hello, guys," he said cautiously. "What are you doing out here in my neck of the woods this time of the night? Is anything wrong?"

Chip breathed a sigh of relief. Sheldon's manner was friendly. "I'm sorry it's so late, Mr. Sheldon, but we wanted to talk to you about the story," he said nervously. "The story about Duck Tucker."

"Sure," Sheldon said quietly. "Come on in."

Mike Sheldon always dreaded the reaction to a scandal story. It usually turned out that someone who had little or maybe even nothing to do with the real cause of the trouble was the person who got hurt the most. He listened to the two boys and resolved to do all he could to help them with their problem. Chip told him little about his own difficulties, but Bobby Barber wasn't so quiet about Chip's plight.

"And they're blaming Chip for everything that's happened! They all saw him talking to you down at the field, and they think he gave you the scoop on Tucker. Remember when you were leaving? When you said the story would be in Tuesday's paper? Then, when Kirk got fired, he told a lot of the workers that Chip, here, was responsible for all the trouble. And they thought you meant the Tucker story."

"I don't care anything about Kirk or Dillon or Duck Tucker, Mr. Sheldon," Chip said earnestly, "but I don't want the men in the Yard to think I'd do a thing like that." He reflected a second and then continued, "I'm not bitter at whoever told you the story either."

"No one told me the story, Chip," Sheldon said quietly. "I got a letter through the mail and checked up on it. Then I had to write the story. This newspaper game, you know, is a tough one. I had no real desire to write this story, but after I was in it— Well, in my business, stories like that don't come along very often, and if I hadn't written it someone else would have.

"I have no idea who wrote and mailed the letter to me, nor why. Probably someone who had it in for Tucker or for the Steelers."

Bobby nodded his head. "Yeah, there's no doubt about that, but look who gets all the blame? Chip! And that's no good! He was a hero until this thing came out, and now, all at once, he's a pariah! And he had nothing to do with it at all. That's what hurts the most! It's just not right!"

Chip had been concentrating on Sheldon's words about the letter. That letter held the key to the whole story. Maybe there was some way they could trace the writer through the letter itself.

"Do you still have the letter, Mr. Sheldon?" he asked hopefully.

"Well, the original is put away at the office. The paper always keeps that kind of letter. I've got a photocopy. Fact is, I've got it right here in the house. In my briefcase. Like to see it?"

Later, when Chip and Bobby left, they took the photocopied letter with them. Sheldon made Chip promise he wouldn't show it to anyone and that he would return it to him before the end of the week.

It was just after 1:00 A.M. when the weary friends piled off the bus in Mansfield, but neither was interested in sleep. They were getting somewhere at last, and they didn't intend to let the clock stop them. They headed for the nearest diner for hot apple pie and coffee. On stools at the end of the counter, they continued their discussion.

"Now, what?" Bobby asked.

Chip had spread the letter out on the counter and was studying it intently. "We've got to find out who wrote this," he said thoughtfully, still studying the letter.

"How you gonna do that? It's typed!"

"Well, actually, that makes it easier. We know it's not done at a computer work station or by a printer. That means it was done on a typewriter, probably electric since I doubt many offices have the old manual ones anymore. And all typewriters are different!"

"No!"

"Yes!"

"How come?"

"Why, they're something like hands. The keys are like fingers and no two of them write exactly alike. It's something like fingerprints."

CLUTCH HITTER

Bobby nodded his head excitedly. "Sure," he said now catching on, "that's right! I remember now! I read about that in a mystery story once. Hey, we're doin' all right!"

"We sure are," Chip agreed. "Look, Bobby, look at each letter *l* in this letter. See? See it there in 'will' and 'dilly.' It shows up better there. See the break in it? That irregular letter *l* proves it's gotta be from a typewriter."

"Yes!" Bobby exclaimed. "It's like that in every one of 'em! Look at 'em. Must be a dozen of 'em. Count 'em!"

Chip counted the *l*'s slowly. "One in July and Sheldon. That's two, three, four, five, six, seven, eight and nine, and two in dilly; that's twelve. There's twenty-three!"

July 29

Mike Sheldon
Sports Department
The Journal

Dear Mike:

Want a story that will splash every sports page in the State? If so, drive over to Glendale this coming Sunday afternoon. There will be a dilly of a semipro ball game at Brook Field between Glendale and Mercer and you'll get a big kick and a bigger story out of the Glendale battery.

A fan who likes clean amateur sports

P.S. Be sure to bring a camera.

"That's right, Chip!" Bobby said. "Twenty-three it is! Never thought about it, but the *l* must be the most used letter in the alphabet!"

"Not quite," Chip said preoccupied. "The *e* is used most, but that broken *l* will sure make our job easier if we can get some letter samples to compare with this one. That's our big job now."

"We'll do it," Barber said confidently. "We've got to do it some way."

Chip examined the envelope and the canceled stamp. "This was mailed from Mansfield on the twenty-ninth of July at 5:30 in the afternoon," he mused. "That means it wasn't a ballplayer because they'd all be practicing unless they got someone else to mail it."

"Why couldn't a ballplayer mail it?" Bobby demanded. "What's the time got to do with it?"

"Well, I'm just surmising, of course, but it seems to me that this letter went out in the regular afternoon mail from some office here in town. You see, most mail goes out the last thing before closing the office for the day, and if some secretary mailed it, the post office time stamp wouldn't get on the letter for quite a while after it was dropped in the mailbox or dropped off at the post office. No, I think it came from some office."

Barber was still puzzled. "What will finding the typewriter the letter was written on prove though, Chip? And how we gonna tell who wrote the letter even if we do find the right typewriter? Anyone could walk into an office and use a typewriter, couldn't they?"

"Sure they could! But we have to start somewhere, don't we? Look, here's what I mean."

Chip pulled a paper napkin out of the counter dispenser and began to write on it.

"Number one! Finding the typewriter will give us the location. Right?"

Bobby nodded somewhat dubiously. Chip continued. "Number two! Knowing the location will make it easy for us to develop a list of people having access to the typewriter.

"Three! Then we can use the process of elimination to get a list of suspects."

Bobby looked at his friend and began to laugh, "You're a real Sherlock Holmes, aren't you? Say, Holmes," he murmured admiringly in a fake British accent, "you astonish me! By the way, old chap, may I call you Sherlock?"

Although he responded with a grin, Chip continued, basically ignoring Bobby. "Four, we can study the phraseology or word choice used in the letter and apply it to the personalities of the suspects."

Barber shook his head in amazement. "Man," he commented, "this gets more intriguing all the time! This is beginning to sound like a John Grisham novel!"

"Five! Then we can check and see what potential suspects had access to that typewriter on the date the letter was mailed. Right?

"Sixth—"

But Bobby had had enough. "I believe you, Holmes," he whispered hoarsely. "What's the next step? Going to sleep, I hope."

"Well, I'd hate to think someone in the plant would pull a nasty stunt like that, but you never can tell. It's the best and most convenient place to start. We've got to get a specimen of the type of every machine in the Mansfield Steel Company offices."

Bobby's eyes opened wide. "Every typewriter in the plant? Hey, why our company? Why, that'd take a week!"

MIKE SHELDON'S STORY

"What else is there to do? Where else can we start?"

Bobby shook his head. "Ya got me," he said dejectedly. "I don't have a clue. Besides it's getting late."

The two boys sat quietly, each busy with the problem. It was Barber who solved it first. "I can do it!" he almost shouted, springing to life. "I can do it! Gimme that letter!"

"How?"

"Can't tell you right now! But I can do it! See you tomorrow in the Yard!"

And with that, Bobby Barber grabbed and pocketed the letter and zipped out the diner door, leaving behind a perplexed Chip Hilton.

CHAPTER 15

Generosity of Spirit

PEGGY ARMSTRONG shifted her attractive brown eyes away from Bobby's imploring gaze. "I don't think I'm interested, Bobby," she said slowly. "As far as I'm concerned, the whole baseball affair is a finished book I'd like to forget and put behind me." She paused and tried to avoid his insistent look, but loyal Bobby Barber wasn't going to be put off that easily.

"Look, Peggy," he insisted, "I've got proof— Well, nearly proof, that is, right here in my pocket that Chip didn't tell Sheldon about Tucker."

Bobby pulled the envelope out of his pocket and showed her the letter. "See?" he said eagerly. "Chip wouldn't be trying to find out who sent this letter if he was guilty, now would he? I mean, the very fact there's a letter proves he didn't tell Sheldon about Tucker when Sheldon was interviewing him, doesn't it?"

A comprehending look coupled with sudden interest flashed across Peggy Armstrong's face. "*Yes,* Bobby, that does seem logical!" Peggy's keen mind began churning.

GENEROSITY OF SPIRIT

"Chip's plenty burned up, Peggy," Bobby said hurriedly, "not only about the way everyone's been treating him, but because the Yard crowd thinks they're going to run him out of the Yard with the treatment. He's determined to find out who sent the letter. You gotta help!"

"All right, I'll help," Peggy said decisively, "if you promise not to tell Chip."

"Don't worry about that. *I'm* not going to tell him! I wouldn't *dare!*"

Peggy scanned his face closely. There was speculation in her eyes. "Why wouldn't you dare tell him?" she probed curiously.

It was Bobby's turn to look down and avoid Peggy's eyes. He cleared his throat and shuffled his feet uneasily. "Oh, you know why, Peggy—"

But Peggy shook her head obstinately. "No, I don't," she insisted. "Why?"

"Aw, you're gonna make me say it, aren't you? I guess it's because he's never gotten over the time you broke that lunch date with us and then, you know, how you acted, remember?"

Peggy's eyes clouded a bit. "Yes," she said reflectively, "I remember, and I've been sorry about that ever since. You mean, then, he wouldn't want me to help out, is that it?"

Bobby nodded his head. "That's about it."

Peggy laid a soft hand on Bobby's arm. "Well, I guess at least you know I'm sorry, and someday I'll get a chance to tell Chip too. Now, let's get started."

That evening, a perplexed watchman kept a discreet eye upon the activities of a strange teenage duo in the offices of the Mansfield Steel Company. The big boss's daughter, along with a brazen, laughing young idiot, tried out every electric typewriter in the building. And even then the picky girl couldn't find one to suit her. All she did was type a few words on each one, but evidently it didn't satisfy her. If she wanted to type something, why not use one of the computers, the watchman wondered. But he wasn't about to say anything to H. L. Armstrong's daughter. He read one of the pages that had slipped to the floor. It consisted of a single sentence: "Mid pleasures and palaces there is no place like home." He scratched his head and tried to figure it out.

It didn't make sense to the watchman, and it didn't add up to anything that helped Peggy and Bobby get any closer to identifying the machine the poison-pen letter had been typed on either.

Chip gathered together the pages Bobby had brought him and sighed with disappointed resignation.

"Well, it looks as though that idea bit the dust. Hey, Barber, how did you get these anyway? You sure you didn't miss any machines?"

Bobby shook his head vigorously. "We didn't miss a one!"

"We?"

"Me! I mean me, I, me!"

"But how did you get them?"

"I got 'em! Isn't that good enough? All I can say is I'm glad Armstrong has been shifting over to word processing, or I'd still be there!"

"Yes, I guess so. Thanks, Bobby. Now, what to do—"

"You know, Chip, it could've been someone at Mackin Motors."

"It could," Chip said dubiously, "but I doubt it."

Bobby bristled a little. "Well," he said firmly, "you yourself said we had to start somewhere and we did! We started in our own plant! Now, we've got to start somewhere else and it might just as well be at Mackin's.

GENEROSITY OF SPIRIT

Besides, they're the team that benefits most from what happened to the Steelers."

Two hours later, Chip and Bobby were still wrestling with the problem of getting at the Mackin typewriters. And they were still struggling with that problem the following evening.

"Looks like we're stopped," Chip said dejectedly.

"Yeah," Bobby agreed. "Peggy doesn't know how we're going to do it either."

"*Peggy!*"

"Man, Chip, I couldn't help it! I had to get those typing samples somehow."

"You mean Peggy Armstrong got those samples?"

"Yep! That she did! We went down to the plant the very next night after you gave me the letter! We worked there until after midnight!"

"And nobody saw you?"

"Sure, the night watchman knew we were in the offices, but what could he do? It was Peggy Armstrong, wasn't it?"

"Yes, but—"

Chip was stunned. Peggy Armstrong had helped get the lettering samples! Why? He hadn't talked to her for over a month. He just didn't know much about girls, that was for sure. It was a pretty great thing for her to do.

While Chip and Bobby were involved in the problem, Peggy Armstrong was puzzling over it too. She was sitting quietly in a big wing chair in her father's study, concentrating for all she was worth.

H. L. Armstrong knew his daughter almost as well as he knew himself, or at least he thought he did. He watched her over the top of his book, noting her preoccupation and closely knit eyebrows. So when a little later Peggy spoke out of the deep silence, he was ready.

"Dad, something's got me stumped."

"That's *something!* What could have *you* stumped?"

"Sort of a problem. Suppose you wanted to get an example of the print from every typewriter in a certain building, and you didn't want anyone to know you were getting them. How would you do it?"

"Your own building?"

"No, the building belongs to someone else."

"What is this, one of those logic quiz problems?"

"No, but it's nearly as bad."

Armstrong pondered the proposition. "I suppose you want to do this in a legal manner," he questioned, "without risking arrest?"

Peggy laughed. "Of course. You wouldn't want me to get arrested for burglary, would you, Dad? That's the tough part of it."

"That *is* a tough assignment," Armstrong said with a warm grin, "but you don't mean to tell me you're going to let a little thing like that stump Rachel Margaret Armstrong? Of course, if I knew more about the problem, I might be able to take care of it for you."

Peggy read the challenge in her father's eyes, and her own brown eyes suddenly became determined. "No, *sir!*" she declared. "I'll work it out all right by myself!"

That night, Bobby led a reluctant Chip Hilton to the library in the recreation building where Peggy was waiting. Chip felt awkward at first, but he soon got involved with Peggy's and Bobby's enthusiastic suggestions for getting the samples from the Mackin building.

"You know," Chip pondered aloud, "we're in a tough spot. We can't expect a Mackin employee to help us, and we don't want to do it ourselves because we'd be trespassing."

"Well, then, let's get someone else to do it!" Bobby said flatly.

GENEROSITY OF SPIRIT

"That's no good," Chip said with a laugh. "We'd still be accomplices and just as guilty as if we did it ourselves."

"That's right," Peggy added. "We have to get someone to do it who has a right to be in the Mackin offices and who still wouldn't be disloyal to Mr. Mackin."

"How about a salesman?" Chip said.

"Yeah!" Bobby echoed. "A typewriter salesman!"

"That could be it, Bobby, but I know dad's buying more computers and printers than typewriters now," Peggy said thoughtfully.

"How about a typewriter service company?" Chip asked abruptly.

"That's it!" Bobby snapped. "That's it!"

"I think that might work," Peggy agreed. "I know the man who takes care of the typewriters for many of the businesses in Mansfield. I think I can persuade him to do it when he knows the whole story and if we promise not to tell how we got the information."

"Assuming we get some information, which I doubt," Chip said.

"Well, you never know until you try," Peggy rejoined. "Give me three days. I'll meet you here Friday night. I think I'll have the samples with me too!"

The next three days dragged for Chip for many reasons. Conditions in the Yard were really getting bad. Chip had great difficulty ignoring the Yard treatment and a couple of times nearly became involved in verbal exchanges. But he managed to keep his head, watching the calendar and hoping something would come of Peggy's efforts. Even those of the Yard men who were most bitter in their feelings toward the "snitcher" admitted that the kid could take it. Chip sensed that Bobby Barber, Jake Miller, and Bert Long were defending him, but he would have been happily surprised had he known that Big Nose and Pig Iron had used their weight, too, to stop the hazing of Chip Hilton. Every day that passed brought him closer to the day he would start back to Valley Falls and school, his friends, and football. If only he could leave Mansfield with his name cleared . . . .

On Friday evening, Chip and Bobby hurried to the recreation building. A demure Peggy Armstrong was there ahead of time, looking prettier than ever, dressed in a light blue that brought out the color of her flawless complexion. Bobby didn't even say hello.

"How'd you make out?" he demanded. "You get 'em?"

Peggy smiled triumphantly. "What do you think?" she asked in a tantalizing voice.

"I think you did it!" Chip declared on a sudden hunch.

Peggy flashed that quick smile in his direction. "You're right," she declared proudly. "Here they are!" She laughed as she whipped the sheets of paper from her shoulder bag.

Chip glanced down at the sheets. Each was nearly filled with the familiar sentence.

"What are the numbers for?" Bobby asked.

"The locations of the typewriters," Peggy said. "See, here's the master sheet that tells us right where every typewriter is located."

"How in the world did you get this?" Bobby asked in a surprised, admiring tone.

Peggy laughed again at the memory. "Oh, just used a little psychology," she said. "Just suggested to Mr. Johnson that it was a *very* important test I was making and that my father was *very* anxious for the test to be successful, and that I would make sure that everything was kept *very* confidential and— Well, that's all there was to it! Come on, let's check them out."

GENEROSITY OF SPIRIT

For the next hour, three heads were bent closely over the pages, each pair of eyes looking eagerly for the broken *l*. It was tedious work, and as page after page disclosed nothing but perfect *l's*, their hopes began to fade.

Then they saw it! All three at once! "There it is!" they blurted out excitedly, almost in unison. "There it is!"

"Compare it with the letter," Peggy said carefully.

Chip spread the letter out on the table and compared the two broken *l's*. "They're identical," he cried excitedly.

Peggy hurriedly scanned the master sheet. "Number 320. Let's see, that came from one of the typewriters in the Mackin main office. Can you imagine that?"

"That doesn't help much," Bobby said mournfully. "But there're a hundred people who work in the main office."

But Peggy was jubilant. "Yes, but don't you see what this letter proves? It proves Chip didn't write it and therefore didn't tell Mike Sheldon about Duck Tucker!"

"Sure! That's right!" Barber affirmed happily. "What's the matter with me? Man, oh, man, won't everybody be glad to hear this?"

"No, they won't," Peggy said in a warning voice. "Remember my promise to Mr. Johnson! Remember, I told him it would be kept confidential. I can trust you, can't I?"

Bobby seriously nodded his head. "Yes, of course, Peggy," he said resignedly. "But I sure wish we could find out who wrote it." He was struck by a sudden thought and turned to Chip. "Say," he sputtered, "didn't you say something about being able to tell who wrote something by the words they used? By the way they wrote?"

Chip nodded reflectively. "Yes, sure, but that only works when you know a lot of people and you are trying to figure out which one it is. I don't know anybody at Mackin's."

Peggy had been listening closely to the conversation. Thoughtfully, she plucked the letter from Chip's hands and concentrated on the words. Halfway through, she snapped her fingers and jumped to her feet. "I've got it!" she let out abruptly. "I know who wrote the letter!"

"Who?" Chip and Bobby chorused. "Who?"

"Why, it was—" Peggy suddenly covered her mouth with her hand, and her voice faded away. Then she shook her head. "I'm sorry," she said slowly. "I'm sure I know who wrote it, but I can't tell."

Bobby gazed at her in amazement. "Why?" he asked. "Why can't you tell us?"

"Because, well . . . just because I can't. I'm sorry. Let me have the letter, Chip. I want to show it to Dad. I'll bring it back to you the first thing Monday morning. And please promise me, both of you, that you won't breathe a word about this to anyone."

Chip and his friend looked at each other with serious expressions and promised Peggy they'd keep quiet.

That didn't stop Bobby from spending the next two hours trying to guess the identity of the writer, but Chip didn't have to do any guessing. He was pretty sure he knew.

Peggy found her father in his study as usual. Without knocking, she burst in on him. "Dad," she cried, "you know the story about Chip, about Chip Hilton? Well, it's not true. He never told Mike Sheldon about Duck Tucker and that Dillon person, and I can prove it!"

"Whoa, whoa, child. What's this all about? One thing at a time. I thought you were so sure the Hilton boy had told the story, thought you had figured him out, so to speak. Now the shoe is on the other foot, eh? How about all the men in the Yard? You mean they're all wrong too?"

"Yes, I do! They're all wrong. You too!"

GENEROSITY OF SPIRIT

"Me?"

"Yes, you! You believed it, didn't you?"

"Wait a minute, Peggy. I never said I believed it. I said I had heard it. Now suppose you tell me what this is all about."

Peggy told her father the whole story. About the letter and her part in getting the specimens from their own offices as well as Mackin's. Then she handed him the Sheldon letter and Mackin specimen number 320.

"See the *l,* Dad? See the cleft in it? In the middle? See, it's in the letter and in the sample too. And," she continued breathlessly, "I know who wrote the letter!" She paused victoriously. "See if you can figure it out."

Armstrong read the letter aloud. But it didn't register. "I don't get it, Peggy," he said. "It doesn't tell me anything—"

"Dad! You don't mean to tell me you can't tell who wrote that letter? Just think a minute. Who does it sound like? Just imagine someone talking and using the words." Peggy paused and then repeated slowly, "Using the words in the letter."

While her father was reading the letter, Peggy began to hum a little ballad he knew he'd heard somewhere before.

Roses are red, dilly, dilly,
Violets are blue,
But my memories are green dilly, dilly,
Of the day I met you.

Halfway through the letter, H. L. Armstrong cleared his throat and glanced sharply at Peggy. "That's a pretty song," he said. "You know, Peggy, I believe I do see it now. The *l's* in the letter and the typewriter specimen *are* identical."

Armstrong paused and brushed his hand thoughtfully across his forehead. Then he hushed Peggy as she started to speak and continued, "And I'm quite sure I see the something you are referring to, but it isn't too obvious, and I believe I'd rather skip it."

Peggy knew her father and knew when to talk and when to share the silence that meant he was deep in thought. Now she sank back in her chair and waited for him to continue. After a short time, he went on with the discussion just as though there had been no interruption.

"Let's think about this a minute, Peggy. Couldn't you call the whole thing to a halt now? Now that you know Hilton is cleared, I mean. I'll see to it that his name is vindicated at the company. I intend to make sure all the men in the Yard know Chip Hilton had nothing to do with the Tucker incident. I'll see to it, personally.

"It seems to me you've accomplished all you set out to do when you found out Chip Hilton wasn't involved. And since that was your goal to start with, I think it would be honorable to let the whole matter drop now, right where it is. What do you say, Peggy?"

Peggy Armstrong knew and loved the side of her father's nature he had just revealed. She knew this side of her father's spirit just as well as she knew her own name. A gentle smile of respect and understanding spread across her face, and her eyes suddenly softened. Yes, Peggy Armstrong knew the generosity that graced her father's spirit . . . knew he was too much of a true man of God to want to hurt someone, particularly if that someone was the son of his best friend.

CHAPTER 16

Poison-Pen Letter

DAVY MACKIN wiggled his driver and then carried it slowly and smoothly all the way back for a full swing. At the top of the stroke, he paused a split second, then sent the club whistling down and out with ever-increasing speed until the graphite head met the ball with a sharp crack. The dimpled sphere was swept away in a beautiful, low-rising trajectory, which labeled it for a good 225 yards.

It was a beautiful drive, even though the fairway was baked a bit dry and the roll added a few extra yards. Most golfers would have felt a glow of pleasure at the oohs and ahs that followed, but Davy Mackin wasn't in the mood to appreciate a good shot. He hadn't even followed the flight of the ball. His hands had followed all the way through and his eyes were still focused on the wooden tee that remained where he had placed it. That was probably the reason the results had been so good.

"That was a beauty, Davy," his father said proudly. "A real beauty! He got hold of that one, didn't he, H. L.?"

CLUTCH HITTER

Armstrong nodded. "He sure did," he said, smiling ruefully. "Guess we should have stayed at home today. Right, Peggy?"

"Yes, it was a *dilly,*" Peggy said pointedly, looking sideways at her father, "a dilly with two *l's!*"

H. L. Armstrong frowned and turned back to Dave Mackin. Peggy was sorry almost as soon as she had made the remark, but she had lost interest in this golf match and in Davy Mackin too. There just wasn't any fun in playing against someone like Davy. She had agreed to play today only because she knew how much her father liked these matches between the two families.

Yes, Davy Mackin was an uninterested golfer that day. He was thinking only of baseball—and the letter! The Mackins had clinched the Mansfield Industrial League championship three days earlier, and last night the team had been the guests of honor at the league banquet.

Davy was thinking about the letter, the letter that had paved the way for his father's team to win the pennant and qualify for the national tournament. This wasn't the first time he had worried about that stupid letter. He had regretted that hasty action many, many times. He felt especially cheap today, playing with the Armstrongs.

What had been the matter with him? Just because a lot of the Mackin employees had listened to his boasting and had done a lot of betting, giving big odds on the Mackins as a no-brainer to win the city championship, there was no excuse for him to cheapen himself by stooping to write a poison-pen letter. He wouldn't have had to write the letter if it hadn't been for the Steelers' new pitcher. And who in the world would have figured Hilton to be that good? Well, the Mackins had won, all right, but they couldn't have done it without that letter.

POISON-PEN LETTER

Davy glanced at H. L. Armstrong. He couldn't help but admire a man like that. He had been so gracious last night when the Mackins were honored. If it hadn't been for the letter, Armstrong and Peggy would have been the hosts at the big party last night, *they* would have heard the mayor praise the Steelers players and everybody connected with the team in those extravagant terms he used, and *they* would be wearing the gold baseball charms.

Davy clamped his jaw savagely, biting down hard on his lower teeth, and swung viciously at the ball. But he hadn't concentrated, and the result was a bad shot. He topped the next, hooked another into the rough, overshot the green, and finally wound up with a bad nine on a par-four hole.

Davy would remember that afternoon for a long time. The game became more unbearable with every hole. It seemed that every bit of conversation was directed toward him, even when his father and H. L. Armstrong spoke of Duck Tucker. Well, a guilty conscience needed no accuser.

"Have you seen Tucker since you fired him, H. L.?"

"Yes, Dave, I have. Fact is, he was in to see me just yesterday. I believe the lesson he's learned may turn out to be the best thing that ever happened to him."

"Guess he'll feel pretty miserable if he goes back to State."

"Yes, I guess he will *if* he goes back. But I expect he'll want to transfer to some other school now. You see, he's lost his athletic scholarship, and no coach at State will let him participate in any athletics after this scandal. He hasn't made up his mind yet about that, but he promised me he would complete all the requirements to earn his undergraduate degree.

"He also apologized to me for his actions. Told me all about the difficulties he had caused for Hilton. About how he burned Hilton's jacket, razzed him, and played dirty tricks on him all through the season. It took guts for him to take the responsibility for all that, Dave. This may be what Tucker needed to make a man of himself. You have to feel sorry for a youngster who has a great future but chooses to throw it away and take the crooked road.

"By the way, Dave, we've learned that Chip Hilton had nothing to do with the story Mike Sheldon printed."

Dave Mackin beamed. "That *is* good news," he said happily. "I was hoping that report about the kid was untrue. He just didn't seem like that kind of person to me. He struck me as the kind of kid who, if he definitely knew something like that was going on, would think about going to the person himself and trying to persuade him to change. He'd probably even stand by him while he did."

"Yes, I think so, too," Armstrong replied. "It seems that someone wrote a letter to Sheldon and told him about Tucker's affiliation with Glendale, and Sheldon investigated and got the whole story."

"Oh, well, it's all over now. Let's get back to this golf game and my beating you. Who's teeing off next?"

On the way home, Davy finally raised the subject that had been gnawing away at him all afternoon. "Dad," he said hesitantly, "can I talk to you about something important?"

"Why, certainly, son. What's on your mind?"

"Dad, I want to talk about the Tucker mess. I know all about it. I ought to—I wrote the letter Mr. Armstrong was talking about."

"*You* wrote the letter?"

POISON-PEN LETTER

"Yes, Dad. I wrote the letter to Mike Sheldon that led to Duck Tucker being exposed."

"But why, Davy? Why?"

"You know, Dad, I really don't know myself. I guess it all goes back to my hoping to win the pennant for you and also to my own crazy desire to be a big shot in the eyes of the men at the plant. I was so sure we'd win that I guess I bragged too much, and the men all bet pretty heavily on us to win. And then when Hilton came along and the Steelers began to win, I just seemed to lose my head."

"But, Davy, I don't understand how you found out about Tucker."

"That was just by chance, Dad. You remember the Sunday afternoon Mom and I drove over to Glendale to see Mrs. Skinner? Well, that afternoon Glendale was playing, and I went to the game, and Tucker and Dillon were there. I asked around and found out they played there every Sunday using phony names, and it made me angry. I'm not trying to excuse my part, Dad, but I wanted them thrown out of the league, and then I thought I could take care of two situations at one time— get them out of the league and clinch the pennant at the same time. Guess I was just about as wrong as they were. They played under assumed names, and I wasn't man enough to sign my name to the letter."

There was a long silence. Dave Mackin automatically slowed the car and tried to figure out his course of action. But it was Davy who continued.

"There's something else I'd like to tell you, Dad. Something about golf. I didn't make a birdie on the third hole this afternoon. I had a four. I'd like you to know I've done that quite a few times, but, well, I'll never do it again! You've got my word on that."

CLUTCH HITTER

Dave Mackin and his son were unusually late for dinner that evening. And it was probably the most important two hours in their lives because the understanding and closeness that resulted from their long talk would remain with them forever.

That evening, H. L. Armstrong was surprised to receive a phone call from Dave Mackin. After he hung up, he turned to Peggy in surprise. "Now what do you suppose that's all about? That was Dave Mackin, and he wants to see me about something important. Maybe you'd better beat it before he arrives, honey."

Dave Mackin and H. L. Armstrong were old friends. Although they were keen rivals in golf and other competitions, beneath their apparent sporting battles was a feeling of genuine friendship and mutual respect. Armstrong knew something was very wrong the moment he met Dave Mackin at the door, and his agile mind immediately sensed that this urgent meeting had something to do with young Mackin.

After they were comfortably seated in Armstrong's study, Dave Mackin surprised his host by abruptly challenging him to a series of baseball games to be played over the Labor Day weekend.

Armstrong studied his friend suspiciously. "What is this, a joke?" he asked with a laugh. "I disbanded my team. You know that."

"I'm serious, H. L.," Mackin said soberly, "dead serious."

"You know what it means if you play us, don't you, Dave? It means your team will be disqualified too. Playing us will eliminate you from the national championships. You can't be serious about this."

But Dave Mackin was serious and after an hour of futile argument, H. L. Armstrong accepted the challenge. "Remember I warned you," he cautioned.

POISON-PEN LETTER

"And don't start crying when the national association pins a year's suspension on your team. Better think twice. A year's a pretty stiff penalty to pay just to play a three-game series with a team that has been disqualified. You've got nothing to gain and everything to lose."

Dave Mackin searched his friendly rival's eyes, shook his head, and then a brief smile flickered across his lips. "I guess you know more about this matter than you let on, H. L., and I guess you understand what I'm talking about when I say there's more to it than meets the eye. And maybe you'll understand me when I say that taking this penalty, a year's suspension, is more important to me than the city championship, the national championship, or anything else."

Armstrong rose and nodded with empathy. "Yes, I think I understand, Dave. I think I understand everything." He grasped his longtime friend on the shoulder. "Now, my fine friend, don't you think we ought to have a little contest on the outcome of the series?"

Mackin was his smiling, jolly self again. "And how!" he agreed. "You name it!"

"Well, how about a big party for both teams and everyone involved at the Buckeye Inn?"

"No entertainment?"

"Oh, sure! A banquet, an orchestra, dancing, and everything that goes with it!"

"It's a deal! We'll complete the arrangements tomorrow!"

At the door, Armstrong placed a hand on Mackin's shoulder. "Dave," he said softly, "it's pretty hard to take when something happens to mar a fine achievement, but there are other things more important than baseball and sports championships. Some ideals that are almost as important as life itself—that *are* life itself."

CHAPTER 17

The Yard Code

CHIP HILTON had never been in H. L. Armstrong's office. Now he stood in the big, oak-paneled, luxuriously furnished room and waited for the big man to speak.

"Sit down, Chip," Armstrong said in a friendly tone. "I've sent for you this morning to let you know that Peggy told me all about the anonymous letter and your, should I say, detective ability. I want to congratulate you on a job well done."

Chip smiled but said nothing. He felt awkward and ill at ease.

"Chip," Armstrong continued, "lots of people make mistakes. I've made many mistakes and no doubt you've made a few too. I know you've had a pretty tough way to go in the Yard, and I can appreciate that you must have had some bitter thoughts about Duck Tucker. But sports and the great athletes who engage in them are not concerned with petty jealousies and minor grudges. I hope you'll forget all about the bad treatment you've received."

THE YARD CODE

Chip sat quietly in his chair, his gray eyes fixed upon the serious face of his employer.

"I have a favor to ask of you, Chip. I want you to do as Peggy and I are going to do. I'd like you to consider forgetting all about the letter and the person who wrote it. I'm certain you know who the author is, and I appreciate your sportsmanship in remaining quiet. I hope you can influence Bobby Barber to do the same. Perhaps it's asking too much, but judging from the splendid way you've weathered the Yard storm, I'm pretty sure you're big enough to do it."

The tall, slender boy's radiant smile told H. L. Armstrong what he wanted to know. He stood up and clapped him affectionately on the shoulder.

"Here's Sheldon's letter. Don't let him worm anything out of you. He's clever! Getting information is his business, and he's pretty good at it. And, Chip, I guess you know what this means to me, and to someone else who went to school with your father."

Chip Hilton jumped to his feet. The look that passed between the older man and the young athlete as they gripped hands was long and full of appreciation.

Bobby was waiting anxiously when Chip returned. "What happened?" he asked. "What'd he want? What'd you say?"

Chip told Bobby all about the conversation and that Armstrong had returned the letter. "He wants us to drop everything and to forget the whole mess ever took place. I gave him my word that we would. That's all right with you, isn't it, Bobby?"

Bobby Barber nodded his head solemnly. "Sure, Chip, if it's all right with you," he said quietly. "But I'd sure like to know who wrote that letter!" He looked at Chip searchingly, a sudden suspicion on his face. "You know, don't you!" he said suddenly.

Chip shook his head. "No, I don't know," he said firmly. "I've got a pretty good idea, but I don't really know and I'd just rather forget it. This isn't just something the big boss is asking us to do, Bobby. It's something . . . it's something my Dad would want me to do too."

"That's OK with me, Chip," said Barber with his best grin. "I never saw any letter. I can't read, and I don't like pictures. I prefer pitchers, if you catch my drift!"

That afternoon after work, Bobby insisted upon practice at Steeler Field. "Jake's coming down to throw a few and I want you to help me with my catching."

"But how about the letter?"

"We'll take it out to Sheldon's house tonight, OK?"

Jake Miller came hustling along almost as soon as the four o'clock siren sounded and joined Chip and Bobby on their walk through the Yard. There were fewer turned heads and no remarks whenever Chip was accompanied by Jake Miller. Long ago, Chip had realized that the friendly Yard boss was going out of his way to be around just at the end of the shift so he could walk along with him and Bobby on their way out of the Yard.

Chip realized, too, that something was happening to the silent treatment. Most of the riding had ceased. Although he had been with the Mansfield Steel Company for nearly two months, he didn't yet know nor understand the iron-bound code of the Yard. The Yard respected guts and strength of character above all, and the kid had shown he had plenty of both. He had never shown the slightest indication that he was going to quit under fire, and he had done more than his share of the hard, grueling labor assigned to the workers.

The older men had appreciated Chip's pitch-in spirit in his work and had relented after the first few days. And, although they hadn't been as friendly as in the past, they now greeted him when they walked by and even stopped to shoot the breeze.

Chip had been surprised, too, several times by a friendly wave from Big Nose when he passed him in the Yard. Once, when he was leaving the main gate, Pig Iron had slapped him on the back with a hamlike hand and said, "Hang in there, kid!"

When the three friends passed the grandstand gate, Chip cast a regretful look at the locked dressing room door. It seemed too bad that the spirit that had just begun to warm that battered room should be lost.

Jake Miller was rapidly getting back in shape. As he and Chip alternated throwing to Bobby, he talked about the days when he had been Chip's age and had dreamed of being a professional pitcher.

"Not that I was ever half as good as you, Chip," Miller said, "but we all have a few dreams, and that was one of mine."

On his next turn to throw, Jake waved his pitching hand from the right side of his shirt to the left and then bent a slow curveball across the outside corner of the plate. Bobby whistled in admiration and gunned the return throw to Chip. "He bent that one, didn't he, Chipper?"

Chip nodded enthusiastically. "I'll say he did! Wish I could control my curve like that!"

He tried the same pitch, but the ball swung wide of the plate. "I can't do it, Jake," he said, shaking his head dubiously. "When I ease up, I lose my control."

"Sure you do," Miller said. "So why slow up? If I had your arm, I wouldn't ease up either. You've got the sharpest breaking hook I ever saw, Chip. It's just as if it drops off a table. Don't you ever ease up on it unless you're way ahead on the count and want to use it for a change-up."

Chip nodded. That's exactly what the Rock had told him too. Still, he had to look up to a pitcher who could control soft stuff. It seemed as if Jake could even ease up on a screwball. Chip had to throw *his* screwball with every bit of speed he had.

Just then, Chip caught sight of several figures filing through the gate by the grandstand and heading down into the dressing room.

"Hey, look," he said, pointing, "there goes Shorty and Don and Joe Ferris. And they're all going down to the dressing room. What's up? And there comes Brad Cooper and Lefty Curtis too. Wonder what that's all about?"

But Miller and Barber weren't interested. "I don't know," Miller said nonchalantly. "Say, I'd like to try that blooper pitch of yours. How do you hold it?"

Chip showed Jake how he held his blooper, but his heart wasn't in it. He had known for days that Bobby, Bert Long, and Jake Miller were protecting him all the time, jeopardizing their own reputations in the Yard by standing by him. All at once he was tired of everything— tired of trying to keep up a good front, tired of the thinly veiled insults, tired of the cutting remarks, tired of the way the guys in the plant avoided him, tired of H. L. Armstrong and the Steelers and the Mackins and Mansfield.

If it hadn't been for Bobby and Jake and Bert and, well, Peggy Armstrong, he guessed he'd have gone home long ago. This was August 30, though, and that meant there were only four more days to go. Then he'd be home with his mom and all the Valley Falls crew. That would be the end of Mansfield forever, as far as he was concerned. The third of September couldn't come too soon for him! That would be Saturday, and he'd decided to buy his ticket tonight on his way back to Mrs. Pecora's. Labor

THE YARD CODE

Day was Monday, and on Tuesday he'd be back in school for his senior year and out for Valley Falls football.

It would be easy to forget Duck Tucker and Gunner Kirk and Buster Dillon and Davy Mackin. But he guessed it would be a long time before he'd forget Bobby Barber and Jake Miller and Bert Long and Peggy Armstrong.

Chip didn't see H. L. Armstrong go through the grandstand gate and down to the locker room or he would have been more than surprised. But he knew just about the whole baseball team, with the exception of Bobby and himself, was gathered there for some unknown reason. And it didn't really matter, after all, if they didn't want him along. Only that wasn't playing fair with Bobby. And what if they did blame him for everything that had happened? At least the people who really mattered knew the truth—at least Armstrong, Bobby, and Peggy knew.

Down under the grandstand, Armstrong waited patiently for the shuffling feet and creaking benches to become quiet as he studied the faces of the players before him. The Steelers were a good-looking outfit, H. L. decided. All the better looking without Gunner Kirk and Buster Dillon! Then he began to speak.

"Men, I guess you were all grievously disappointed because of the unfortunate incident that occurred two weeks ago. Certainly, it was a shock to me. I am truly sorry that we didn't look after Tucker a little more carefully and that we didn't check the characters and backgrounds of Kirk and Dillon more thoroughly. That was my mistake. My own daughter told me Kirk was a rotten manager. I should have taken her tip. But I promise you it won't happen again."

At this admission, several players laughed. When all was quiet again, Armstrong continued.

CLUTCH HITTER

"I know you feel the same way I do about withdrawing from the league. I'd be ashamed to win any championship under false pretenses, and I'm glad the matter came out before the season ended. I would never have forgiven myself if we had gone on through the season and won the city championship, and maybe the national championship, only to have it come to light that we won with a team carrying professionals. Boys, we were lucky."

H. L. stopped to look carefully at each serious face surrounding him. "But that's over, for good, I hope. Amateur sports are too big and too important for incidents like the one we've just been through to handicap them much, and that's the way it should be."

He paused again and scrutinized the sober-faced group. His eyes showed his pleasure as he noted the players' reactions, and he was proud that such a clean group of men represented his company. He smiled and continued.

"I've decided to go ahead with the team, men. We've been busy all day arranging details for a three-game series with the Mackins to start next Saturday."

It took only a second for the players to grasp the significance of Armstrong's words. Then they nearly lifted the grandstand with their yells. When they quieted, Armstrong continued.

"Best two of three. First game to be played this coming Saturday afternoon, and two next Monday afternoon, Labor Day. And they're all to be played at the City Stadium."

Armstrong didn't have to be told that the team liked that announcement. Their shouts and cheers nearly blasted him out of the room. Their big boss was some guy! Oh, boy! So Armstrong and Mackin were at it again! There was something behind this! Armstrong had probably needled Dave Mackin about the best three out of five the Steelers had won from the Mackins and the way the kid had set them on their ears!

It was too bad about the kid. He could really throw 'em in! Bet Mackin had gotten good and sore! The Old Man had a way about him! Always seemed to get the best of Mackin even when the Steelers got whipped! Well, they wouldn't let the Old Man down! If only that Hilton kid hadn't gotten mixed up in the Tucker trouble.

Almost as if he had read his players' thoughts, Armstrong began talking about the very athlete they were all thinking about. "Men," he said in a serious voice, "there's something else that is even more important right here at this point. It's about the pitcher most of you refer to as the kid—Chip Hilton!

"Hilton has experienced a pretty raw deal through circumstances he had absolutely no control over. Practically everyone in town has believed the ugly and unfounded rumor that it was Hilton who told Mike Sheldon about Duck Tucker's pitching for the Glendale Bears and getting paid on the side for it. I have to admit I fell for the circumstances, too, just as some of you did. But we were all wrong, and Hilton and one other person were the only people in Mansfield who knew the truth.

"I guess we all know how rough the Yard can be when someone gets out of line. And, I still remember what that Yard Court is like. Not many boys, or men either, can take the going-over that crowd gives you. But Hilton did, and I'm sure glad he did! We would all have felt pretty awful if Hilton had quit and gone back home and then the truth was found out, as it now has been. Thank goodness he's not the quitting kind!

"Through all this, Hilton stuck to his job and his principles without saying a word in his own defense. He took everything the Yard could throw at him and came back for more. When all that time he didn't have a thing to do with the Tucker affair. Not a single thing!

"Furthermore, he took a lot from Tucker, Kirk, and Dillon. Most of what I'm trying to tell you I learned first-hand from that threesome. But I learned much more about the Tucker angle from several other individuals who were in a better position to know *all* the details. I'm proud that we were fortunate enough to have the best pitcher in the state playing for us this summer, and I hope he'll be back for many more summers. Oh, I nearly forgot. Jake Miller will be back with the team. Curtis, ask Miller, Barber, and Hilton to come in here, will you, please?"

Lefty Curtis surprised Chip when he suddenly appeared in the dressing room doorway and bellowed, "The Old Man wants to see you three in here right away!" But he didn't surprise Barber, Miller, or Long; they'd been waiting for this! And it was worth waiting for! That morning in his office, Armstrong had made all the arrangements for this surprise for Chip when he had called Jake Miller at the Yard.

Chip was surprised again when he entered the dimly lighted locker room and was greeted by the smiles and friendly winks of the players. Armstrong briefly reviewed what he had just said about the arrangements for the series and then reached a big hand down to grasp Chip's and haul him to his feet. Then, placing his other hand on Chip's shoulder, he continued, "There's one thing more I'm sure you men will appreciate. I want you to meet Chip Hilton, your new Steelers playing-manager!"

Armstrong had thought that first cheer was something, but the one that followed his latest announcement made the first seem like a whisper. Several of the players jumped up and grabbed for their bewildered new manager's hand. Others began pummeling him on the back. The warmth was back in the Steelers locker room.

The new player-manager of the Steelers was too overcome with the big boss's announcement to do anything more than stammer a few words that nobody heard. All he could think of in that shouting, laughing, pushing madhouse was, "If only the Rock were here to tell me what to do!"

"Chip," H. L. Armstrong was talking again as the room quieted down, "I don't know how you're going to get by with only *one* pitcher and *no* catcher, but I guess that will have to be your problem. Oh, yes, by the way, I am in full sympathy with your resolve not to pitch without three days' rest. I'd have been most disappointed in you if you had let Hank Rockwell, your coach and my friend, down by breaking your promise to him. There are thousands of youngsters who have ruined a great baseball career by showing off and abusing their arms. So don't get the idea I expect you to pitch more than one of those games."

Chip smiled and then winked twice. Once at Jake Miller and once at Bobby Barber. "I have a couple of ideas about the pitching and catching, Mr. Armstrong," he said. "I think I know where there's a pretty good battery just waiting for an invitation to show their stuff!"

CHAPTER 18

Third-Strike Bunt

MIKE SHELDON, grumbling and without his usual sense of satisfaction, ripped the sheet of paper from the printer and studied the story that would appear in the Tuesday morning *Journal.*

MACKINS TO PASS UP NATIONAL AMATEUR ASSOCIATION TOURNAMENT CHALLENGE STEELERS
Mackins Anxious to Prove Superiority

By Mike Sheldon

Dave Mackin, president of Mackin Motors, announced today that the Mackin Motors baseball team will not compete in the national amateur baseball championships, which will begin in Louisville,

THIRD-STRIKE BUNT

Kentucky, next week. Instead, the recently crowned city champions will jeopardize their newly won honors by engaging the Mansfield Steelers in a three-game series starting on Saturday, September 3. The first game will be played Saturday afternoon, followed by a double bill on Labor Day afternoon at City Stadium.

The announcement brings to a head the rumors that have been flying about the city ever since the Mansfield Steelers withdrew from the league three weeks ago. At that time, the Steelers had virtually clinched the pennant.

When asked why his team was not entering the national championship tournament, Mackin stated that he was more interested in local sports than in the national limelight and that he and his team were influenced in making the decision because they had practically backed into the championship because the Steelers had withdrawn from the city league. The Steelers forfeited all their victories following the exposure of a prominent member of their pitching staff who was participating as a professional with the Glendale Bears.

The Mackins' decision to play the weekend series against the Steelers may well mean the Mackins will join the league's erstwhile leaders as an independent amateur baseball organization. The Steelers were declared ineligible to compete against member teams of the national association for a period of one year.

It's well known in Mansfield sporting circles that Dave Mackin would rather win a sports contest from H. L. Armstrong than win an Olympic medal.

Due to the superb pitching of Chip Hilton, the Steelers bested the Mackins in the city league regular schedule, winning the last three games after losing the first two they played.

H. L. Armstrong, president of the Mansfield Steel Company, announced that William "Chip" Hilton, star Steelers hurler, would serve as player-manager during the series. Hilton, who will graduate from Valley Falls High School next June, reports back to school and football immediately after the holiday.

Sheldon wasn't satisfied. The story lacked something. Just what it was, he didn't know, but he knew that something was missing. Well, he'd think about that, and come Saturday, he'd arrive a little ahead of time at City Stadium to see what he could uncover.

Mike Sheldon had lots of company Saturday afternoon, September 3. The Steeler-Mackin baseball games were grudge matches and always sellouts so far as those two companies' employees were concerned, but they seldom attracted a capacity crowd of nonpartisan spectators. Today, however, was different. Long before one o'clock, no one could get near City Stadium.

City Stadium was the pride of Mansfield. Situated on the outskirts of the city, it was easy to reach by car or bus. The grandstand housed modern dressing rooms, and everything was meticulously maintained. Usually, fans could find a parking place fairly near the ballpark, but not on this Saturday. Cars were parked on the streets and in the driveways for blocks. It didn't seem possible that the stadium could hold all the people who had driven their cars much less those who had walked or come by bus.

Steelers fans were curious about the battery that would face the Mackins. They scanned the squad, trying to figure out the new lineup. Hilton would pitch, of course! And the rest of the roster, with the exception of the catcher, was just the same as the one that had played so well before the incident involving Tucker and Dillon. They looked for a strange face, but the only addition to the Steelers was Jake Miller, and everybody knew he was no catcher! Who was going to do the receiving?

Spectators followed hitting practice, checking the batting order that began to appear on the scoreboard in center field. As names were flashed on the big board, they read them aloud.

WELCH	OK! Shorty was leading off and playing second base as usual! OK!
FERRIS	Sure! Joe was batting second! Joe was the best shortstop in town!
MURPHY	Yep! That was easy! Good old dependable Matt was hitting third and covering the center-field position! Good! Hey! Look! Check that out!
HILTON	Can you imagine that? The kid's put himself in the cleanup spot! And him a pitcher!
COOPER	Something wrong here! Brad's batting fifth, huh?
CURTIS	Ah, Lefty! The finest first baseman in amateur baseball and the nicest guy! Bar none!
ARMEDA	Pete "the Arm" Armeda was hitting in the right position anyway! Seventh! Now for the catcher! Maybe Barber was receiving! He was wearing a catcher's glove!
CATOLONO	No! That can't be! Don's no catcher! Something's wrong! Well, maybe the kid's

making the catcher—whoever he is—hit last!

MILLER   Hey, what goes? Miller? Why, he hasn't played all year! He can't catch anyway! Say, who is going to catch this game?

A murmur went up from Steelers fans, but they forgot the catching problem as they watched the names of the Mackin players begin to appear, one by one, on the other side of the scoreboard. A rousing cheer from the huge Mackin rooting section accompanied each name.

SHARP   Sure! Good right-field throwing arm! Good leadoff man!

JONES   Uh-huh! Good push-along guy! Good shortstop!

RICE   He's a bad-news guy! Covers center field like a blanket! What he hits is considered lost and gone!

LEMLER   Natch! The greatest long-ball hitter in the state! And the best left fielder too!

WILSON   And how! An artist around the hot corner! Hard hitter! Good competitor!

BENSINGER   The Keystone kid himself! Smart! A hustler! A real holler guy if there ever was one!

GALLAGHER   Good hit! No field! When he's at bat, duck!

HOUGHTON   Dillon number two. Good catch! Good hit!

KURT   The master! Yep, the guy with the nothing ball you still couldn't hit!

As the last name went up, Steelers fans shook their heads, and their eyes shifted doubtfully across the board to their own lineup. Uh-uh! This didn't look too good! The Mackins had a tough, experienced ball club! They were out for blood too! Anyone could see that! They were burning.

No sir! Things didn't look so good! No Dillon! No Tucker! No Kirk! No experienced manager! No reserve pitchers! Sure, the kid could throw and he could hit! But managing? That's a whole other matter. And if Hilton pitched today, who was going to pitch the Monday games? Hadn't that been one of the big differences between Kirk and Hilton? Hadn't Hilton said all along he wouldn't pitch more often than every three days? Sure, Miller had pitched last year, but he hadn't been playing and wouldn't be able to hold the Mackins down with that worn-out arm of his. Even if he did, who would pitch the third game?

Steelers fans were correct about the arguments between Chip and Kirk concerning pitching. But they would have been amazed at the arguments Chip Hilton, the pitcher, had been having with Chip Hilton, the manager.

Chip Hilton, the pitcher, had been firm in the promise he had given to the Rock, for the protection of his arm. Chip Hilton, the manager, had been all for winning the series at any cost.

Chip had held strategy practices every day and had tossed restlessly every night, trying to figure out what he was going to do about pitching and catching. He could and would go one game, but how about the other two? Jake Miller could go one, maybe, but Chip had never seen Jake pitch. Besides, Miller hadn't pitched for nearly a year. Suppose either or both of them got into trouble! What then? He might be able to relieve in one of the Monday games if he pitched the first game, but he couldn't go the route in two of these games and still hold to his promise to Rockwell.

CLUTCH HITTER

Of course, Armstrong had said he was glad Chip had held his ground about pitching only after three days' rest, but there was more at stake now. There was a team of really good guys to think about. And there was Chip Hilton's responsibility as Steelers manager to think about too.

At the first practice, he had been nervous and worried about how the team would react to following his leadership. Not that he hadn't led teams before, but this was different. This was a team of men instead of high school athletes. It meant a lot to him that Mr. Armstrong had that much confidence in him, but he wasn't sure how his teammates would react to his new position as player-manager.

He soon found out, however, that he didn't have to worry. Lefty Curtis, the man every player and every Armstrong employee respected highly, settled that even before Chip had a chance to talk. Curtis stood up and said, "Chip, the whole group has asked me to act as their spokesman. We want you to know that we're solidly with you 100 percent. We think you're a great pitcher and a great guy. We know just how you feel about taking the manager's job. We had a little meeting all our own last night and voted you our full support. You make the decisions, and we'll back you up!" Curtis had smiled then and added, "Now, does that make you feel any better?"

It sure had! What a switch—the players were giving their manager a pep talk. Chip had needed those words of support. He planned his campaign carefully just as Rockwell used to plan for an important game. Then he talked it over with the team in the strategy meetings. The most important problem was, of course, the pitching. That had Chip stumped. But it didn't have the team stumped. Jake Miller took the initiative.

THIRD-STRIKE BUNT

"Chip," Miller said, "I've been away from the team for a year, and maybe I'm speaking out of turn, but I'd like to make this suggestion. Let me pitch, or try to pitch, the first and third games. I know just what you're thinking. You're thinking about breaking your promise to your coach out of loyalty to us, without the three-day rest. Well, we all agree with your coach and with H. L. Armstrong about that decision, and we're not going to let you take a chance on hurting your arm. Bobby Barber can catch, and I'll pitch the first and third games if you want to go along with that. I'm all washed up anyway!" He chuckled grimly. "I can't hurt my arm!"

Chip had decided to go along with the plan for Miller to pitch the first and third games, but he reserved his decision about the catching. Pete Armeda said he had caught when he was a kid on a Little League team, and Bobby thumped his catcher's glove and looked at Chip suggestively.

So now, just before game time, the team—and everyone else—was surprised when Chip, wearing a catcher's glove, walked out to the plate to take part in the infield warm-up.

Peggy Armstrong, her father, Dave Mackin, and a subdued Davy Mackin watched the game preparations from a box on the third-base line, speculating about the Steelers' battery. Peggy was the first to figure it out. "Dad," she said excitedly, "I'll bet you Chip Hilton is going to catch!"

"Oh, I don't think so, Peggy," Armstrong replied. "Hilton isn't a catcher. Even if he could catch, I don't think he'd risk it. It's too dangerous; he might ruin his pitching hand."

But Peggy was right. When the umpire called, "Play ball!" the battery was Miller and Hilton.

CLUTCH HITTER

The stands buzzed. Say, this kid was all right! Imagine that, he puts himself in the cleanup spot in the batting order, and now he's going to catch! Hope he knows what he's doing! This isn't playground ball!

Chip soon demonstrated that he knew what catching was all about. His throws to second were fast and right on the bag. And that wasn't just pregame stuff either! He threw just as well under pressure, what pressure there was. Jake Miller's soft stuff was working beautifully. The Mackin batters were trying to tee off but were getting absolutely nowhere. Chip and Miller worked perfectly together, and the Steelers and their supporters immediately got behind them.

Lefty Kurt was just as effective for the Mackins. Inning after inning of the scoreless game sped by. Before the fans realized it, the seventh-inning stretch had come and gone, and it was the last of the ninth with the Steelers at bat.

Shorty Welch was a good leadoff man and proved it by working Kurt for a free ticket to first base. And true to form and baseball batting orders, Joe Ferris dropped a bunt down the first-base line, and Shorty was on second with one away.

A hit could win this game now, and Chip, on deck and swinging two bats, gave Matt Murphy the hit-away sign. Matt got under one and lifted a high fly to the right-field fence. Everyone in the park saw Bob Sharp set himself just short of the fence for the long throw to third, and the whole Steelers bench was yelling to Welch, "Tag up, Shorty, tag up!"

Lefty Curtis, in the third-base coaching box, cried, "Go! Go!" just as the ball met Sharp's glove, and Welch did just that, beating the perfect peg by ten feet. And now it was two away with the winning run on third base. Any kind of a hit would break up the game. It was a perfect spot for a clutch hitter!

Chip, batting righty against Kurt's left-handed breaking pitches, stepped up to the plate. Kurt had kept everything low against Chip all afternoon, and he did the same now, bending pitches around the knees and working the count to two and two. Chip figured Lefty would try to slip this next one by and got set. Kurt tried and nearly did it! The ball swooped in, just outside the corner. Chip, with his heart in his mouth, let it go, and the count was three and two.

All the fans in the stadium were on their feet, adding their voices to the deafening roar. Chip stepped out of the box. He leaned his bat against his thigh and rubbed his hands across his shirt to wipe off the salty perspiration. All the time his thoughts were racing. Bunt on the third strike? What a crazy thought! But crazy stuff sometimes won ball games. He glanced at the Mackin infield, playing deep, playing for the third out. It might work! But if he missed it or bunted it foul for the third strike, he'd be laughed out of town!

Chip called time and walked slowly behind the catcher to the other side of the plate. He was cool and calculating now. The decision had been made. Batting left-handed, he was thinking, *I'll be closer to first, and I'll try to drop one down the third-base line and beat it out.*

Lefty Kurt smiled. The kid was looking at that right-field fence. Good! He'd get him now!

Kurt spun a wide curveball, low and away from the plate. Then Chip shocked Lefty Kurt and everybody else by stepping forward and dropping a perfect bunt down the third-base line. Hug Houghton, the Mackin receiver, was caught by surprise, and Lefty Kurt was completely flat-footed on the mound. He didn't even field the ball.

CLUTCH HITTER

Shorty Welch unleashed a shout of surprised glee and was home before the base umpire had called Chip safe at first. Then Chip was mobbed by his teammates and, out on the scoreboard, a big black "1" flashed into the Steelers' ninth-inning score frame. The game was over. The Steelers had won the first game of the series, 1-0—on a third-strike bunt!

"On a what?"

"You heard me! The Steelers won the game on a third-strike bunt!"

CHAPTER 19

The New Manager

MIKE SHELDON had been writing for the *Journal* for more years than he liked to remember, and he'd been present at most of Mansfield's Labor Day sports events. But he had never seen a crowd as frenzied as the one that had elbowed and pushed its way into City Stadium on this Labor Day. It was the largest and the loudest Mansfield crowd he had ever seen.

Mike wiped the perspiration from his forehead and gazed down at the playing field from his perch in the press box. The first game of the doubleheader had just ended, and now he could sit back and relax with a cool drink and ponder the game he had just seen, as well as think about several things he just couldn't figure out about this Mackin-Steeler series.

What was this all about? Why would Dave Mackin want to play the Steelers instead of taking his team to Louisville and playing in the national championships? It just didn't add up! There had to be something else that he was missing!

And the game that had just ended didn't make sense either. Hilton had pitched near-perfect ball, the Steelers had hit the ball hard, had played flawlessly in the field, and still they had lost the game. Mackin's Red Corrigan had bested Hilton in a pitchers' duel and had won by a score of 1-0.

But the score didn't tell the true story. Hilton had struck out twelve Mackins, hit three for three at the plate, and pitched well enough to win any game. In fact, the game had been lost after Hilton had struck out three men in the bottom of the ninth. With Jones, the Mackin shortstop, on second base, two down, and the count on Lemler three and two, Hilton had sidearmed his fastball around Lemler's wrists for the third strike. Lemler had missed the blinding fireball by a mile, but so had Bobby Barber!

The ball had sped through Barber's hands and clear back to the grandstand with the new catcher chasing to pounce on it like a cat. But it had rebounded crazily away, eluding Barber's desperate lunge and spun into the Mackin dugout. Tough break? Sure! But that was baseball!

At any rate, it had set things up in fine style for the second half of the twin bill and the series' payoff game coming up. Now what would the young kid manager do? Call on Miller again and resume his catching as he had in the first game? Or would he pitch two games the same day? And if he did, would the kid catcher, who had just cost the Steelers the game, work behind the plate again?

The answers weren't long in coming. When the Steelers took the field, it was Miller on the hill and Bobby Barber back behind the plate. Some Steelers fans didn't like that, maybe because of their loyalty to the team and maybe because of the wagers they had made with the Mackin crowd. They let Chip know it too.

"What is this? More three-day stuff?"

"Get Barber out of there, Hilton!"

"Give us a break, kid! Pitch it yourself!"

But Chip was sticking to his plans, and the Steelers players were sticking with him. Jake Miller and Bobby Barber gave Chip and the team everything they had on every pitch. It was a brutal game, another pitchers' battle. Lefty Kurt and Jake Miller matched cunning and experience right down to the wire.

The Mackins scored two in the seventh, and the Steelers came right back and tied the game in their half. In the eighth, the Mackins scored two more. But this time, the Steelers got only one back, and there it stood until the bottom of the ninth when the formidable Kurt's support slipped. Lefty Curtis drove a hard grass cutter far to Jones's right, and the Mackin shortstop made the mistake of trying the long throw. The ball sailed over Gallagher's head, and Curtis scampered on down to second base.

Armeda sacrificed Curtis to third and was out at first. Catolono met Kurt's first pitch, pulling a sharp ground ball directly at Wilson who was standing on the baseline between second and third. It should have been an easy out at first, but the ball took a bad bounce and slipped right past Wilson. Jones, the Mackin shortstop, backed up the play and made the stop, holding Curtis on third and allowing Catolono to reach first.

Now it was one down with the tying and winning runs on first and third, and Bobby Barber was up. Bobby hadn't hit a ball all day, and besides, he was dead tired. The crowd was in a frenzy, and Chip, sitting in the dugout, experienced his first bit of indecisiveness as a manager. This called for a pinch hitter. But he had a hunch on Bobby. Bobby was due! He was overdue! Chip was partly right. Bobby Barber was past due, but he went down swinging with all his might on three straight strikes. Catolono had taken advantage of Kurt's absorption with Barber to skip down to second. And now Jake Miller was up.

Up in the press box, Mike Sheldon sighed and shook his head in disbelief. How about this? Three games and every one nip-and-tuck right down to the wire with an exciting, heroic finish all set up for the last inning. It didn't seem possible, but here it was again. One run behind, two down, runners on second and third, and a pitcher who hadn't played ball for a year in the hero spot!

"Maybe this is what Dave Mackin meant," Sheldon muttered over his laptop. "Maybe the guy's got something with that local competitive angle. Just look at this crowd!"

The young manager of the Steelers had known this moment was going to come up in the series—a situation in which Chip Hilton would have to make a decision that would mean victory or defeat. Now he could really appreciate a baseball manager's problems: when to yank a pitcher, when to put in a pinch hitter, when to play for a single tally, to squeeze in a run, or to go all out for the big inning. He wished the Rock was here now.

Lefty Curtis was perched on third with the tying run, and Catolono was standing on second base with the winning run. What a spot! Last of the ninth, two down, runners on second and third, and the score 4-3 against the Steelers.

Jake Miller took a long time choosing a bat. Jake was tired. His thin shoulders sagged with weariness, and there was a questioning look in the eyes he turned to Chip for instructions.

THE NEW MANAGER

Jake was game! He'd try! But he hadn't come near the ball all day, and Jake and everyone else knew that this was it! That it had to be now or never! Jake and everyone else knew that a pinch hitter was the play. Any kind of a hit would bring Curtis in and maybe Catolono too. Catolono could run with the best of them.

Streaking through Chip's thoughts ran the Rock's admonitions about pitching: "Promise me you'll never pitch two days in succession, never pitch unless you have three days' rest." Well, he hadn't gone back on his word yet, but if he went in for Miller and only one run scored, he'd have to break that promise. How about someone else? He knew the answer to that one before he turned to look at his group of tense teammates. That was out! There *wasn't* anyone else! There was only one logical person . . . only one person who could make *this* decision. Chip Hilton!

For just the briefest part of a second, Chip hesitated as foreboding thoughts rushed through his mind. He'd been blamed for losing the second game, razzed for using Bobby, and criticized for not pitching two of the three important games. If he fizzled out in this clutch spot, he'd *never* live it down.

That challenge did it! Chip reached Miller's side in one long stride. "I'll hit, Jake," he said softly. "I can do it! I've *got* to do it!"

Chip took his time getting up to the plate. Above the din of the crowd, he heard the umpire shout, "Hilton now pinch hitting for Miller!" He stopped just short of the third-base side of the batter's box and knocked an imaginary bit of dirt from the spikes of each cleat. Then he yanked his helmet down over his left eye and stepped up to the plate. His heart was pounding as it had never pounded before. He almost believed he could even hear it above the thumping sound of the Mackin catcher's fist in his glove. He had made this decision; now he had to make it stick. A hit of any kind could make up for the disappointment of the last game. But that was beating a dead horse. It was over and finished. He had to get on with this game. This was his chance!

Lefty Kurt had pitched a hard game, and the stocky southpaw was tired. He shot a quick glance beyond the Mackin dugout where Red Corrigan, the tall, lanky hero of the Mackins' victory in the previous game, was throwing leisurely. But there was no sign from the Mackin dugout, and Kurt sighed and stepped to the mound. But he didn't like this spot and stepped right back down off the mound. He was careful to step straight back and to make no motion of any kind; he couldn't afford to commit a balk now.

Kurt was reviewing the Saturday game in his mind, the game Hilton had won with his third-strike bunt. Kurt had been tricked then. He wasn't going to take any chances now. He was going to be ready for a bunt this time.

Again Kurt looked for help, but the Mackin manager made no move, and Lefty toed the rubber. He took his stretch, lowered his hands, came to the required stop, glanced toward Curtis on third, and then broke one of his darting curveballs around Chip's knees. But it was inside and ball one.

Chip stepped away from the plate and again went through his batting ritual, knocking the red clay from each shoe and yanking his helmet a little lower over his left eye. Then he stepped back into the batter's box. But Kurt was through. The Mackin manager called time, and Red Corrigan came walking slowly out to the mound.

Chip stepped back out of the box, then walked behind the umpire and to the other side of the plate. There was a murmur from the stands when the crowd realized that

THE NEW MANAGER

Chip was going to switch hit. He was going to hit left-handed against the tall right-hander.

Corrigan took his warm-up pitches, and Chip, standing nearly back to the on-deck circle, ripped his bat through several times with a full left swing. With the umpire's "Play ball," Chip shifted his helmet to the right and down a bit over his right eye, tapped each shoe, and stepped into the box.

Corrigan sized Chip up and took the sign from his catcher. Then he toed the rubber and extended his arms at full length over his head. Standing motionless, Corrigan shifted his eyes from Chip at the plate to Curtis on third base. Lefty grinned and danced his feet in a sign of support. However, the lanky first baseman was careful not to stray too far from the sack.

And it was a good thing he didn't because Corrigan suddenly threw to the bag. It was close, but the base umpire flattened the palms of his hands. Chip breathed a sigh of relief. Corrigan took the return throw from Wilson and promptly blazed it back in an attempt to catch Curtis napping. But Lefty had learned his lesson. He was only a short step away from the bag.

Then Chip decided he could play cat-and-mouse, too, and he stepped back out of the box. While Corrigan was waiting, Chip went through his painstaking batting ritual again and feigned extreme anxiousness. But it was all a fake. Chip had decided to take one to get a look at Corrigan's stuff. Corrigan took his stretch, eyed Curtis again, and then snapped a sharp, darting slider that caught the inside corner belt-high. It was a called strike, and Chip regretted his decision. He liked that kind of ball. But the opportunity was gone, and the count was one and one.

Chip was tempted to outguess Corrigan, to figure out the next pitch. But he hastily put that out of his mind.

He had tried that at other times, and it always got him into trouble. He'd look 'em over as they came.

Corrigan was taking no chances. He blazed his fastball around Chip's knees, and Chip reluctantly let it go by for another called strike. It seemed to Chip then that every fan in the stadium was on his case.

"Get that stick off your shoulder!"

"What's the matter, Hilton? Hypnotized?"

Chip was out of the box now and trying to calm his nerves as he tapped each shoe with his bat. He felt as though he didn't have strength enough to lift the bat, to say nothing of swinging it. He'd have to be careful now. Corrigan was ahead of him and far too clever to serve up anything good.

Chip banged the plate hard, and the vibration of the bat seemed to bring life and strength back to his arms. The ballpark was suddenly quiet, like the heavy silence that settles just before a violent storm. For a split second, Chip fancied he could hear the thump-thump of his heart. He listened intently. Why . . . why, this was crazy stuff! Of course he couldn't hear his heart beating!

That little lapse in concentration was nearly disastrous. Corrigan fired one toward the inside corner, and it came whistling in across Chip's wrists before he could move. He tried to pull back, but the ball caught just enough of the handle to recoil over the catcher's glove hand and back to the screen.

Wow! Man! That was too close for comfort! That could have been the ball game.

CHAPTER 20

Clutch Hitter!

DAVE MACKIN glanced sideways at his son. Davy was leaning forward, elbows on the ledge of the box, watching every move Chip Hilton made. Davy caught the movement of his dad's head and turned at the same time. As the eyes of father and son met, a smile of tacit understanding brightened their faces. Each knew what the other was thinking; they were both pulling for Chip Hilton to win this game. And each knew the other was getting a kick out of the reversal of their usual competitive feelings. Imagine! Rooting for the other team! For their opponents to win! But they wanted to square the matter some way, make things right, and that might help a little to wipe the slate clean, help clear their memories of poison-pen letters and conveniently forgotten strokes on the golf course.

Peggy Armstrong, her father, Dave Mackin, and his son were sharing their usual third-base field box and, to anyone watching them, were their usual laughing, joking selves. But the four were forcing their usual enjoyment.

CLUTCH HITTER

Peggy was thinking about Davy Mackin. Somehow, he was different; she had noticed the change in him in a number of ways. It was unusual for him to be so subdued. Surly? Yes! But serenely quiet? Almost peaceful? No! But Peggy Armstrong liked this new Davy Mackin. She liked him so much that she surprised Davy—and nearly herself—by flashing him a warm, genuine smile and by starting a real conversation with him.

Mike Sheldon was still wrestling with the question he'd been troubled by ever since Dave Mackin had announced his team would not compete in the national championships. Sheldon focused his attention on the box where Mackin was seated. For a short time, he was oblivious to the noisy crowd, the time-out down on the field, and the boisterous cries of the vendors parading up and down each aisle selling hot dogs, popcorn, and soft drinks. He had to solve this mystery.

Sheldon saw Peggy Armstrong lean over and touch Davy Mackin lightly on the arm. Sheldon's sharp eyes narrowed for an instant. Then he surprised Bill Andrews of the *Courier* by suddenly snapping his fingers and nearly shouting, "That's it! Now I've got it!"

Andrews regarded him curiously. "Got what?" he asked.

Sheldon laughed shortly. "Skip it, Bill," he said apologetically. "The heat's got me!"

But it wasn't the heat. It was the disappointment that Mike Sheldon felt when he saw the seed of a good story fading away in the heat waves of that September afternoon. He shook his head in disgust, chiding himself for his stupidity. Imagine overlooking the boy-girl angle! He *must* be slipping! No wonder Mackin didn't want to offend Armstrong and vice versa. Those two old buzzards were doing a little matchmaking, trying to fix up their two kids! That was all it was. End of the big mystery.

CLUTCH HITTER!

Down on the field, the Mackins had broken up their huddle behind the pitcher's mound, and the umpire was calling, "Play ball!"

While the Mackins had been talking in their huddle, Chip had tried to figure out what they were arguing about. He felt sure they were debating an intentional pass so there would be a play at any base. And he felt sure Red Corrigan wanted to pitch to him, to win the game with a strikeout. While Chip waited, he covertly glanced at the right-field wall and cautioned himself not to try to kill the ball.

"Just meet it with a smooth swing and a last-second wrist snap," he said so emphatically under his breath that, for a moment, he thought he'd spoken out loud.

He opened his stance just slightly so he could pull the ball and gazed directly into Corrigan's eyes. The challenge he flashed toward the tall right-hander was accepted, and Corrigan blazed a screwball toward the outside corner. If it had been a little higher, Chip might have gone for it, but it was low, and the count was two and two.

Chip stepped out of the box and took a deep breath. Corrigan was going to pitch to him, but he was sure he wouldn't get anything good to hit at. He sure couldn't afford to go for a bad one now, and he couldn't afford to pass up a close one either.

Chip steadied his bat, holding it almost motionless, and waited for the pitch. Corrigan took his stretch and then used all his height to drill an overhand fastball around Chip's wrists. Chip met the ball right on the nose, pulling it just a little. Before he had dropped the bat, he knew he didn't have to run that one out. That one was over the fence, and the ball game—and the Steeler-Mackin series—was good as over.

CLUTCH HITTER

But Chip made sure to step firmly on first base, and so intense was he in his desire to win this game that he tagged each base, concentrating on that detail just as he concentrated when he kicked a placement in football. He watched Lefty Curtis and Catolono too. He wanted to be sure they also gave home plate a solid thump with their spikes.

And then the crowd was piling out of the stands and onto the field, and the whole Steelers team was waiting for him at home plate. Chip Hilton didn't have a chance to walk wearily and happily off that field! And the fans didn't have a chance to get to him either! Before either could happen, he was picked up and carried proudly toward the dressing room by Bobby Barber and Lefty Curtis, Jake Miller and Don Catolono, Joe Ferris and Shorty Welch, Brad Cooper and Matt Murphy, and just about every other player who could get near enough to help.

And while he was sitting up on the shoulders of the men, Chip saw Big Nose and Pig Iron and Bert Long and the rest of the Yard crew yelling and escorting Peggy Armstrong, H. L. Armstrong, Dave Mackin, and young Davy Mackin across the diamond. And the Armstrongs and the Mackins were cheering and waving at him just as happily as his teammates and all the Steelers fans who had swarmed down on the field.

Chip was going to remember the Buckeye Inn for a long time. Any party that Dave Mackin sponsored was good. This one was stupendous. And that wasn't all! The guest speaker was one of Chip Hilton's best friends! The Rock! What a surprise! Coach Henry Rockwell had driven in from Valley Falls to visit his old friend, H. L. Armstrong, and to join in honoring the Steelers baseball team and Chip Hilton. There were a lot of speeches, but

CLUTCH HITTER!

Chip knew he'd always remember two of them, Bobby's and Coach Rockwell's.

Actually, Chip didn't hear Bobby Barber's first words. Neither did anyone else! For the first time in his life, that talkative, loyal friend was having trouble with his speech. Chip was glad of that, too, for it gave him a chance to clear his throat and still his shaking hands. Then, as the last patter of applause died away, Chip heard Bobby's voice. It was clear and sure now—clear and strong and proud.

"And we all got together and bought a present for you, Chip, and, and we all hope you like it, like it as much as we like and respect you. Here, here—Come up here."

Barber was saved further embarrassment by the roar of approval that drowned out his words. A cheer of enthusiasm and joy, which seemed strong enough to shake the rafters, filled the room and echoed through the clean evening air.

"Speech! Speech! Yea, Chip! Yea, Hilton!"

"Go get 'em, kid."

"Yard Court, Yard Court!"

Chip was pushed to his feet and he was shaking Bobby's hand and feeling the warmth of that smile, which he had learned to understand and love in the short time he had spent with this fine friend. He wanted to say something, just anything to express his feelings and his thanks for the privilege of being one of the crew, but the words wouldn't come. This time it was Chip who was saved by the crescendo of cheers.

Everyone was standing and cheering and laughing and applauding and that gave Chip a chance to collect his wits and swallow the lump that was choking off his breath. All the time he was clutching the gift box that Bobby had thrust into his hand.

Then Bobby was gripping his arm tightly and saying, "Look, Chip, Look! Look what's printed on the back."

Chip turned the watch over and there was the inscription:

CHIP HILTON
The Clutch Hitter

The only sound in the car that was carrying Chip and Coach Rockwell back to Valley Falls was the steady purr of the motor. There hadn't been much conversation so far on this trip. Both Chip and his coach were deeply absorbed in their own thoughts.

Rockwell was thinking about the opening of school and the first football practice the next afternoon. And he was wondering if the Big Reds could successfully defend their state championship title.

Chip was thinking about the Yard workers and the team. About Big Nose and Pig Iron and Bert Long and Jake Miller and Bobby Barber . . .

And about Peggy's warm brown eyes . . .

Without warning, out of the comfortable silence, Rockwell elbowed Chip and barked, "Look here, young man, tomorrow's the first day of school and the first day of football practice. Don't think just because you ran that Steelers baseball team that you're going to boss my football team around! Today you were a baseball manager, but tomorrow you'll be a candidate for the quarterback job! I said candidate! Get it?"

Chip leaned his head back against the cool leather seat and deeply breathed in the crisp night air. The nearer they came to Valley Falls, the satisfaction he was feeling about the way things had turned out in Mansfield in his summer adventure was replaced with an excitement churning just below the surface. An excitement about football and new adventures ahead. Chip smiled and regarded his coach with deep respect.

He got it, all right; he knew the Rock. The Rock wasn't letting anyone move in on his job as long as he could walk. And Chip Hilton wasn't letting anyone move in on his quarterback job either.

• • •

Chip's in his final football season at Valley Falls High School and Coach Rockwell's in the hospital fighting for his life.

Be sure to read *A Pass and a Prayer,* the next exciting story in Coach Clair Bee's Chip Hilton Sports Series.

more great releases from the

Chip Hilton Sports Series

by Coach Clair Bee

The sports-loving boy, born out of the imagination of Clair Bee, is back! Clair Bee first began writing the Chip Hilton Series in 1948. During the next twenty years, over two million copies of the series were sold. Written in the tradition of the *Hardy Boys* mysteries, each book in this 23-volume series is a positive–themed tale of human relationships, good sportsmanship, and positive influences— things especially crucial to young boys in the '90s. Through this larger-than-life fictional character, countless young people have been exposed to stories that helped shape their lives.

WELCOME BACK, CHIP HILTON!

TOUCHDOWN PASS - #1

0-8054-1686-2

CHAMPIONSHIP BALL - #2

0-8054-1815-6

STRIKE THREE - #3

0-8054-1816-4

available at fine bookstores everywhere